Folk Tales of the Scottish Highlands

Volume 1

Of Magic, Monsters, and Mayhem

Edited and revised, with notes and an Introduction by

Clayton MacKenzie

Also in this series:

Folk Tales of the Scottish Highlands, Volume 2

Copyright © 2024 Short & Sweet Productions Ltd, London

All rights reserved.

No part of this book may be reproduced, or stored in a retrieval system, or transmitted in any form or by any means, electronic, mechanical, photocopying, recording, or otherwise, without express written permission of the copyright owner.

No responsibility for loss occasioned to any person or corporate body acting or refraining to act as a result of reading material in this book can be accepted by the Publisher or by the Author.

Cover design by: Canva Graphic

Printed in the United States of America

About this book...

The Scottish Highlands, with their mysterious waters and brooding mountains, forever remind us that fairies, giants, and mermaids once also called this place home. Sometimes stirring, sometimes brutal, sometimes hilariously implausible—the stories in this anthology are a treasure house of old and wondrous imaginings.

A group of talking animals mentors a wimpy king; a child is abducted by fairies and a surly counterfeit left in his place; a Spanish princess is rescued from sexual slavery by a Highland tourist; a deadly quarrel is resolved through a game of shinty; a man falls into a nest of savage birds but finds the canniest of ways to survive. These are just a few of the storylines gifted to us from the lips of ordinary folk who lived two hundred years ago. They are stories of their time but their inner voices speak, as well, of the ageless failings and triumphs of human nature.

The tales are edited and revised versions of traditional oral tales, selected from J F Campbell's *Popular Tales of the West Highlands* (1860-62).

Prof Clayton MacKenzie holds a PhD in Literature from Glasgow University. He has led major academic units at universities in the UK, Australia, Hong Kong, and the Middle East. His more than 80 publications have appeared in presses and journals of international reputation. Prof MacKenzie is married with 4 grown-up children.

CONTENTS

Introduction	1
The Young King of Easaidh Ruadh	5
The Smith and the Fairies	21
The Barra Widow's Son	27
The Ridire of Grianaig and Iain the Soldier's Son	43
The Story of the Conall Guilbeanach	67
The Story of the King of Spain	107
The Daughter of the Skies	111
The Daughter of King Underwaves	119

For Moira

INTRODUCTION

More than 160 years ago a set of Scottish tales was published by John Francis Campbell. *Popular Tales of the West Highlands* is a four-volume anthology, gathered from multiple sources by Campbell and, in most cases, translated from the original Gaelic. These were oral tales told by ordinary West of Scotland folk who had heard them from other storytellers, often decades before. Campbell's initial volumes were published in 1860-62; a new and somewhat revised edition was published by the Alexander Gardner Press in London, under the auspices of the Islay Association, in 1890.

The present anthology offers a selection of these tales, with the language and phraseology modernized to make the stories more accessible to contemporary audiences, particularly younger readers. This is always a contentious process and care has been taken to preserve as far as possible the tenor, intention, and spirit of the original text. As often happens with oral tales, there are occasional narrative inconsistencies (for example: competing texts; confused pronouns; plot line non-sequiturs; and spelling variations) which have been amended or adjudicated as sensibly as I can.

Coming from the lips of ordinary people, who lived two centuries before us, these stories resonate with an extraordinary power and connection. They capture a rich life of fairies, spirits, giants, mermaids, monsters, kings, queens, knights, shape-changing beings, violent confrontations, deceptions, supernatural powers, murders, talking animals, reversals of death, magic elixirs—and all manner else of rarefied experiences. Most of all, these are stories that keep us on the edge of our seats, hoping and fearing, as all good folk tales do. They are of their time but they speak also to the inner voices, the secrets and shames and triumphs of our own age.

The tales are marked by unrelenting twists and turns and, in many cases, the gradual knitting together of seemingly unrelated minutiae that is a hallmark of great oratory. The reader is constantly confounded by the intricacy and ingenuity of the storyteller's art. At the heart of that process is the moral imperative that good must triumph over evil. But, truth to tell, it is sometimes an overly convenient good and a begrudgingly exquisite evil. The messaging is not always as clear and straightforward as we might think. And sometimes it is mysteriously challenging, as in "The Daughter of King Underwaves," an enigmatic story from South Uist.

As with any oral tradition, there are sometimes alternative versions of stories and meandering plot lines that seem to drift from their original purpose. "The Story of Conall Guilbeanach," from a storyteller in Dunoon, is a masterly narration. A young royal sets off to find a wife for himself but by the end of the story, after a litany of adventures and misadventures, the quest has dissipated into different territory. But the narration is none the worse for it. We may think of our own histories and remember one or two burning imperatives that somehow faded from importance. The story reminds us (if, indeed, reminding is necessary), that sometimes life just does not pan out as expected.

Magic of some kind is present in every story. "The Barra Widow's Son" is the most haunting and powerful of these; and "The Smith and the Fairies" the most hilarious. Animals that can talk are common currency in these tales, but none is more impudent than the raven in "The Ridire of Grianaig and Iain the Soldier's Son." Similarly, intelligent animals are the saving grace of the fearful king in "The Young King of Easaidh Ruadh." Indeed, in "The Daughter of the Skies" a beautiful young woman wisely chooses to marry a spell-bound dog. But, then again, if you are looking for a story of a man who falls into the nest of giant, savage birds called dreagans, and somehow manages to survive, there can be no more entertaining and implausible account than the "Story of the King of Spain."

Patriarchalism is an unfortunate typification of many of the stories. All too often, women are spoken of as the chattel of men—a commodity to be won, earned, stolen, carried off, or traded. That presumption is outrageous, and it is certainly more than a surface veneer in these stories. But, without excusing this shortcoming, there is a case for arguing that the real power and wisdom in many of these stories is vested in women, specifically in their intellectual wisdom and practical sense. Often it is they who come up with the astute intuitions, the smart ideas, the cerebral insights, and the kinds of nifty work-arounds that rescue the hides of their luddite menfolk by turning near disaster into victory.

My father was born on the Black Isle, near Inverness, in a small croft somewhere in the Strathconon Valley. He was steeped in the traditions of Highland folk and fairy tales and, as children growing up far from Scotland, we were entranced by the stories he told us. Oral narration is a highly theatrical experience and that is hard to convey through black marks on white paper. As readers, this is a limitation we must accept. Stories are not merely to be recited; they are to be performed. There are many instances in the narratives in this anthology when words and actions seem far-fetched. But if, in the dark of winter, we were sitting around a peat fire in a croft, the necromancy of a skilled storyteller might just persuade us differently.

Prof Clayton MacKenzie
Perth, Western Australia

April 2024

THE YOUNG KING OF EASAIDH RUADH

After he assumed the throne, the young King of Easaidh Ruadh was much into merry-making, satisfying his pleasures, and doing whatever caught his fancy.[1]

There was a Gruagach[2] near his dwelling, who was called Gruagach Carsalach Donn.[3] The king thought to himself that he would play a game[4] with him. He went to the soothsayer[5] Seanagal and said to him:

"I've decided I shall go to game with the Gruagach Carsalach Donn."

"Aha!" said Seanagal. "Are you such a man? Are you so bold that you would play a game against the Gruagach Carsalach Donn? I advise you to change your mind and not to go there."

"I won't change my mind," said he.

---

[1] The story is as told in Gaelic by James Wilson, blind fiddler, Islay, 9 June 1859, and written down by Hector MacLean, schoolmaster, Islay. An old man, by the name of Angus MacQueen, who lived at Ballochroy (a megalithic site in Kintyre on the Argyll peninsula), near Port Askaig, told the story to Wilson at some point in the 1820s.
[2] fairy spirit or hobgoblin
[3] a brown, curly, long-haired spirit
[4] It is not clear what kind of game this would be. It is likely to have been cards or dicing, but could also have been billiards, drafts (checkers), or even wrestling. See *Scottish Gaming Folklore and History*, 'https://kilts-n-stuff.com/scottish-gaming-folklore-and-history/', 18 February 2018.
[5] fortune teller

"Then it is my advice to you that, if you should win the game against him, you should name the cropped, rough-skinned maid who is hidden behind his door as the wager for your gaming. He will twist and turn many a time before he agrees to that."

The king lay down that night and, if it was early that the day arose, it was earlier still that the king arose to go gaming against the Gruagach.

When he reached the Gruagach, he blessed the Gruagach, and the Gruagach blessed him.

Said the Gruagach: "Oh young King of Easaidh Ruadh, what brought you to me today? Will you game with me?"

They played a game, and the king won.

"State the stake of your gaming so that I can get on my way," said the Gruagach.

"The stake of my gaming is that you give me the cropped, rough-skinned girl that you have behind your door."

"Many a fair woman have I within besides her," said the Gruagach.

"I will take none but she."

"Blessing to you and a curse on whoever taught you," said the Gruagach. They went to the house of the Gruagach, and he set in order twenty young girls. "Now take your choice from amongst these," he said.

They presented themselves, one after the other, and every one of them said: "I am the one; are you not silly that you are not taking me with you?" But the Seanagal had asked him to take none but the cropped, rough-skinned girl, who would be the last one to come out.

When the last one came out, the young king said "This is mine."

He left with her. When they were some distance from the house, her form altered from a cropped, rough-skinned girl into the loveliest woman the king had ever seen. The king carried on towards home full of joy at choosing such a charming woman. He reached the house and he went to rest. If it was early that the day arose, it was earlier still that the king arose to go gaming with the Gruagach.

"I must go to game against the Gruagach today," said he to his wife.

"Oh!" said she. "That's my father, and if you go to game with him, take nothing for the stake of your play except the dun[6], shaggy filly that has the stitch saddle on her."

The king went to meet the Gruagach, and the blessing of the two to each other was no different from what it was before.

"Yes!" said the Gruagach. "How did your young bride please you yesterday?"

"She pleased fully."

"Have you come to game with me today?"

"I came for such." They began at the gaming, and the king again beat the Gruagach on that day.

---

[6] dull greyish-brown color

"State the stake of your gaming, and be sharp about it," said the Gruagach.

"The stake of my gaming is the dun, shaggy filly with the stitch saddle." They went away together to the stable. The Gruagach brought the dun, shaggy filly out. The young king put his leg over her and she turned out to be the swiftest of heroines! He raced home. His wife spread her hands to welcome him, and they were cheery together that night.

"I would rather," said his wife, "that you do not game with the Gruagach anymore. If he wins, he will bring trouble on your head."

"I can't agree to that," said he. "I will go to play with him again today."

He went to play with the Gruagach. When he arrived, he saw that the Gruagach was seized with joy.

"Have you come once more?" he said.

"I have come." They played the game, and, as cursed fate would have it, the Gruagach won that day.

"Name the stake of your game," said the young King of Easaidh Ruadh, "and don't be hard on me, for I could not bear it."

"The stake of my play is," said he, "that I place crosses and spells on you such that the cropped, rough-skinned creature, who is more uncouth and unworthy than you, should sever your head and your neck, and the very life of you—unless you secure the Glaive[7] of

---

[7] In Gaelic, glaive simply means sword. The Glaive or Sword of Light is a

Light for me from the King of the Oak Windows."

The king went home, heavily, poorly, and gloomily. The young queen came to meet him, and she said to him, "Mohrooai! My pity! There is nothing with you—you seem lifeless tonight!" Her face and her splendor gave some pleasure to the king when he looked on her brow, but when he sat on a chair to draw her towards him his heart was so heavy that the chair broke under him.

"What troubles you so much that you might not tell me?" said the queen. The king told her what had happened.

"Ha!" said she. "Why would you worry about that since you already have the best wife in Erin, and the second-best horse in the kingdom? If you follow my advice, you will come well out of all these things."

If it was early that the day came, it was earlier still that the queen arose, and organized everything—for the king was about to go on a journey. She set in order the dun, shaggy filly, on which was the stitch saddle, which now sparkled with gold and silver. The queen kissed the king, and wished him victory in his quest, and he mounted the filly.

"I need not be telling you anything," she said. "Take the advice of your own she-comrade, the filly, and she will tell you what you should do." He set out on his journey, and it was certainly not dreary to be riding on the dun steed. She would catch the swift March wind

---

familiar trope object that appears in several Irish and Scottish Gaelic folk tales. It is often the subject of a quest in which the hero must embark on a journey to obtain or recover it, or else lose the woman he loves. Such swords are often held by giants, witches, or high-ranking persons of ill repute, and obtaining them is extremely arduous. Often the hero is put in the position where he must secure the sword or else die trying.

that would be before, and the swift March wind behind would not catch her.

At the mouth of dusk and darkness, they came to the court and castle[8] of the King of the Oak Windows.

Said the dun, shaggy filly to him: "We are at the end of the journey, and we will not go any further. Take my advice, and I will take you to the Glaive of Light of the King of the Oak Windows. And if it comes to you without scrape or creak, it is a good omen for our journey. The king is now at his dinner, and the sword is in his chamber. There is a knob on its end. Grasp the knob and draw it softly out of the window."

The young king went to the window where the sword lay. He reached in and caught hold of the knob and it came with him softly until the sword was at its very tip. And then, unfortunately, there was a strange sort of groan.

"We will now be going," said the filly. "This is no time for us to be hanging around. I know the King of the Oak Windows has felt us taking the sword out." The young king kept the sword in his hand, and they went rapidly on their way. After they had traveled some distance, the filly said: "We will stop now, and you must look behind to see what's coming."

"I see," said the king, looking behind him, "a swarm of brown horses coming madly towards us."

---

[8] The court consisted of friends and functionaries of the monarch—often numerous, such that some might need to be housed outside the castle's immediate precincts. Hence the distinction between court and castle.

"We are swifter ourselves than these," said the filly, and they easily outran the brown horses. They went on, and when they had traveled a long way, the filly spoke again.

"Look now. Who do you see coming?"

"I see a swarm of black horses coming towards us. And there is one white-faced black horse, coming in madness—and a man is riding him."

"That is the best horse in Erin; it is my brother, and he received three months more nursing than I did. He will come past me with a whirr.

"Do your best to ready yourself," the filly continued, so that when he comes past me, you will be able to slash the head off the man who is riding him. At the moment he passes, the man will look at you. There is no sword in his court that will take off his head except for the very sword that is in your hand."

Sure enough, when this man was going past, he turned his head to look at the young king. It was the King of the Oak Windows. The young king drew the sword and slashed his head off, and the shaggy, dun filly caught it in her mouth.

"Leap on the black horse," said the filly, "and leave the man's carcass where it fell. Go home as fast as the black horse will take you. I will join you as soon as I can."

He leaped on the black horse, and, "Moirë!"[9]—the horse was the swiftest of heroes! They reached the house long before daylight. The

---

[9] The Gaelic version of Moira. For no obvious reason, it is here used as an expression of amazement.

queen had been without rest until he arrived. But when he did, they raised music and they forgot their woes.

The next day, the young king said to his wife: "I am obliged to go to the Gruagach to see if my spells have been loosened."

"Keep in mind that today it will not be the usual Gruagach who will meet you," said his wife. "He will be furious and wild, and he will say to you, *Did you get the sword?* And you will say that you have it. He will say, *How did you get it?* And you will say, if it were not for the knob that was on its end, I would not have got it. He will ask you again, *How did you get the sword?* And you will say, if it were not for the knob that was on its end, I would not have got it.

"Then he will lift his head to look at the knob on the sword, and you will see a mole on the right side of his neck. Stab the point of the sword into the mole; and if you do not hit the mole, then you and I are both finished.

"His brother was the King of the Oak Windows," she explained, "and he knows that, unless his brother had lost his life, he would not part with the sword. The death of the two of them is in the sword. There is no other sword that will touch them but this one."

The queen kissed him, and she called on victory to be with him on the battlefield, and he went away.

The Gruagach met him in the very same place where he was before.

"Did you get the sword?" he asked him gruffly.

"I got the sword."

"How did you get the sword?" he fumed.

"If it were not for the knob that was on its end, I would not have got it," said he.

"Give me the sword so that I can look at it," he commanded.

"It was not a requirement that I should do so."

"How did you get the sword?"

"If it were not for the knob that was on its end, I would not have got it."

The Gruagach lifted his head to look at the sword; the young king saw the mole. He was sharp and quick, and he thrust the sword into the mole, and the Gruagach fell down dead.

When the young king returned home, he found his set of keepers and watchers tied back-to-back, and his sweetheart wife and the dun, shaggy filly had been taken away.

When he had untied his servants, they told him a great giant had come and he took away the young king's wife and two horses."

"Sleep will not come on my eyes nor rest on my head until I get my wife and my two horses back."

Having sworn this, the young king immediately began his journey. He picked up the tracks of the horses and followed them diligently. Though dusk and darkness were setting in, no stop did he make until he approached a small forest called the Green Wood. He saw where there were signs of a campfire, and he decided to light his own fire in the same place and spend the night there.

He was not long here at the fire when Cu Seang[10] of the Green Wood came to him.

He blessed the dog and the dog blessed him.

"Oov! Oov!" said the dog. "Bad was the plight of your wife and your two horses here last night with the big giant."

"It is that which has set me so urgently and painfully on their track tonight, but it is what it is—there is no help for it."

"Oh! king," said the dog, "you must not be without meat."

The dog went into the woods. He brought back prey, and they feasted together contentedly.

"I am thinking to myself," said the king, "that I should return home; I cannot face that giant."

"Don't do that," said the dog. "There should be no fear in you, king. Strength will come to you. But you must not be here without sleeping."

"Fear will not let me sleep without a guarantee of safety."

"Go to sleep," said the dog, "and I will guard you."

The king stretched out at the side of the fire, and he slept. When dawn came, the dog said to him, "Rise, king. Eat some morsels of meat to strengthen you, and then you can get on with your journey.

---

[10] a dog with supernatural powers

"Now," the dog continued, "if you encounter hardship or difficulty, call for my aid, and I will be with you in an instant." They left a blessing with each other, and the young king departed.

In the time of dusk and gloom, the young king came to a great precipice of rock, and there once again was the remains of the site of a fire. He gathered dry fuel to make his fire. He began to warm himself, and it was not long before the hoary hawk of the grey rock came to visit him.

"Oov! Oov!" said the hoary hawk of the grey rock. "Bad was the plight of your wife and your two horses last night with the big giant."

"There is no help for it," said he. "I have got much of their trouble and little of their benefit for myself."

"Catch courage," said she. "You will get something of their benefit yet. You must not be without meat here," said she.

"There is no means for me to get meat," said he.

"We will not be long without meat," said the hawk. She went off and soon returned with three ducks and eight blackcocks[11] in her mouth. They prepared and cooked their food, and feasted well on it. "You must not be without sleep," said the hawk.

"How shall I sleep without a guard over me, to keep me from any evil that may be here?"

---

[11] black grouse.

"Go to sleep, king, and I will guard you." He let himself down, stretched out, and he slept.

In the morning, the hawk set him on his way. "Any hardship or difficulty that you encounter, at any time, just call out to me and I will come to your aid." He went swiftly, sturdily, on his way.

The night was coming again, and the little birds of the forest of branching, bushy trees were talking about the briar roots and the twig tops; and if they were, it brought stillness but not peace for the king.

He came to the side of a great river and there, on the bank of the river, were signs of a campfire. The king soon turned a little spark into a healthy fire.

He was not long there when a brown otter came out of the river to keep him company.

"Och! Och!" said the otter, "Bad was the plight of your wife and your two horses last night with the giant."

"There is no help for it. I got much of their trouble and little of their benefit."

"Catch courage! Before mid-day tomorrow, you will see your wife. Oh king, you must not be without meat," said the otter.

"How is meat to be got here?" said the king. The otter went into the river and soon returned with three salmon, and they were splendid. They cooked the salmon and feasted.

Said the otter to the king, "You must sleep."

"How can I sleep without any guard over me?"

"Go to sleep, and I will guard you." The king slept. In the morning, the otter said to him, "On this very night you will be in the presence of your wife." He blessed the otter.

"Now," said the otter, "if difficulty falls upon you, just call for my aid and you shall have it."

The king traveled until he reached a huge rock. There was a chasm in the rock and he looked down into it. At the bottom, he saw his wife and his two horses, but he had no idea how he could get down there. He searched until he came to the foot of the rock, and saw a path leading into the chasm. When his wife saw him, she began crying.

"Ud! Ud!" said he. "This is bad! Now, why would you be crying when I have gone to all this trouble to find you?"

"Oo!" said the horses. "Set the king in front of us, and no harm will come to him as long as we are here."

His wife made a meal for the young king and told him the story of what had happened. After they had spent time together, she put him in front of the horses for protection.

When the giant came back, he paused and said: "The smell of a stranger is within this place."

Said she: "My treasure! My joy and my cattle! There is nothing but the smell of the litter of the horses."

After a time, the giant went to give food to the horses, and the horses attacked him, and looked as though they wanted to kill him. He was barely able to crawl away from them.

"Dear thing," said she, "if you are not careful, they may kill you."

"If I had my soul to keep, they would have killed me long ago."

"What do you mean?" she asked. "By the books, I will take care of it."

"My soul is in the bannock stone[12]," the giant confided. When he left the next day, she cleaned and polished the bannock stone thoroughly.

In the time of dusk and lateness, she set her man, the young king, in front of the horses again. On his return, the giant went to give the horses food and they menaced him once more.

"Why did you set the bannock stone in such good order?" said he.

"Because your soul is in it."

"I perceive that if you knew where my soul is, you would give it much respect."

"I would do so," said she.

"It is not there," said he. "My soul is in the threshold[13]." She cleaned and set in order the threshold finely on the next day. When the giant

---

[12] A bannock stone is a D-shaped, flattened piece of sandstone, used for baking scones or bannocks (a flatbread) from oats, barley, or peasemeal.
[13] entranceway of a dwelling

returned, he went to give food to the horses, and the horses threatened him again.

"What brought you to set the threshold in good order like that?"

"Because your soul is in it."

"I perceive if you knew where my soul is you would take good care of it."

"I would do that," said she.

"It is not there that my soul is kept," said he. "There is a great flagstone under the threshold. There is a wether[14] under the flagstone. There is a duck in the wether's belly, and an egg in the belly of the duck, and it is in the egg that my soul is."

When the giant went away the next day, she and the young king raised the flagstone and out jumped the wether and ran off.

"If I had that slim dog of the Green Wood," said the young king, "it would not take him long to catch the wether and bring him to me." The slim dog of the Green Wood appeared suddenly with the wether in his mouth.

When they cut open the wether, out flew a duck on the wing, with other ducks following.

"If I had the hoary hawk of the grey rock," said the young king, "she would not be long bringing the duck to me." Almost instantly, the hoary hawk of the grey rock came with the duck in her mouth. When

---

[14] castrated ram or goat.

they split the duck to take the egg from her belly, the egg popped out and mischievously rolled into the depths of the ocean.

"If I had the brown otter of the river," said the young king, "she would not be long bringing the egg to me." The brown otter emerged from the waters with the egg in her mouth.

The queen immediately took the egg and crushed it between her hands. At this very moment, the giant was on his way back in the early evening darkness. When she crushed the egg, he fell dead, and he has remained so ever since.

The young king and his wife took with them a great deal of the giant's gold and silver. They passed a cheery night with the brown otter of the river, a night with the hoary hawk of the grey rock, and a night with the slim dog of the Green Wood. They came home and prepared a hearty hero's feast, and they were lucky and well-pleased after that.

THE SMITH AND THE FAIRIES

Years ago, there lived in Crossbrig a blacksmith by the name of MacEachern.[15] This man had an only child, a boy of about thirteen or fourteen years of age, cheerful, strong, and healthy.

All of a sudden, the boy fell ill, took to his bed, and moped whole days away. No one could tell what was the matter with him, and the boy himself could not, or would not, tell how he felt. He was wasting away fast; getting thin, old, and yellow.

His father and all his friends were afraid that he would die.

The boy remained in this condition for a long time getting neither better nor worse, always confined to bed, but with an extraordinary appetite.

One day, while sadly reflecting on these things and standing idly at his forge, with no heart to work, the smith was agreeably surprised to see an old man walk into his workshop.

This was a man well known to him for his wisdom and his knowledge of out-of-the-way things. Straight away, he told the old man about the occurrence concerning his son which had clouded his life. The old man looked grave as he listened; and after sitting a long time pondering over all he had heard, he gave his opinion thus:

---

[15] The tale is from the Rev. Thomas Pattieson, Islay. The story was submitted by Rev. Pattieson to the original editor, John Francis Campbell. *Popular Tales of the West Highlands* (Edinburgh: Edmonston and Douglas 1860-62, 4 vols.) without indication of its source. Campbell notes a wonderful and famous history of sword-making on the Isle of Islay.

"It is not your son you have got. The boy has been carried away by the Daoine Sith,[16] and they have left a Sibhreach[17] in his place."

"Alas! And what then am I to do?" said the smith. "How am I ever to see my son again?"

"I will tell you how," answered the old man. "But, first, to make sure that this is not your son, you have got to collect as many empty eggshells as you can find. Go with them into the room, spread them out carefully in front of him, then proceed to draw water with them, carrying them two by two in your hands as if they were a great weight. And then arrange the full eggshells with every sort of earnestness around the fire."

The smith accordingly gathered as many broken eggshells as he could find, went into the room, and proceeded to carry out all his instructions.

He had not been long at work before there arose from the bed a shout of laughter, and the voice of the seemingly sick boy exclaimed: "I am now 800 years of age, and I have never seen the like of that before!"

The smith returned and told the old man.

"Well, now," said the sage to him, "did I not tell you that it was not your son? Your son is in Brorra-cheill in a digh[18] there. Get rid of this intruder as soon as possible, and I think I may promise you your son.

---

[16] Descendants of the Tuatha Dé Danann ("People of the Goddess Danu"), a race of deities that figures prominently in Celtic mythology.
[17] An evil–tempered changeling left in the place of a stolen child.
[18] A round green hill that is frequented by fairies.

"You must light a very large and bright fire in front of the bed on which this stranger is lying. He will ask you *What is the use of such a fire as that?* Answer him at once, *You will see that presently!* And then seize him and throw him into the middle of the fire. If it is your son you have with you, he will call out for you to save him; but if not, this thing will fly through the roof."

The smith again followed the old man's advice, kindled a large fire, answered the question put to him by the boy, and then seized the child, flinging him without hesitation into the fire.[19]

The Sibhreach gave an awful shriek and sprung through the roof, leaving behind a smoldering hole with smoke pouring out of it.

The old man informed the smith that his son was being kept by fairies at a place called the Green Round Hill. This place only opened up on a certain night of the year. On that night the smith, having provided himself with a bible, a dirk[20], and a crowing cock, was to proceed to the hill. He would hear singing and dancing and much merriment going on, but he was to advance boldly. The bible he carried would be an assured protection from any danger from the fairies. On entering the hill, he was to position the dirk in the threshold, to prevent the hill from closing up on him.

"And then," continued the old man, "on entering you will see a spacious apartment before you, beautifully clean. There, standing far within, working at a forge, you will see your son. When you are

---

[19] Fire was an ancient Celtic test for and expunger of evil. During the festival of Bealtain, mentioned elsewhere in this anthology (see Note 50), it was a practice to drive cattle through fire to protect them from evil for the rest of the year.
[20] dagger carried by Scottish Highlanders

questioned, say that you have come to seek him and that you will not leave without him."

Not long after this, the time of the hill opening came around, and the smith sallied forth, prepared as instructed. Sure enough, as he approached the hill there was light, where light had seldom been seen before. Soon after a sound of piping, dancing, and joyous merriment reached the ears of the anxious father on the night wind.

Overcoming every impulse to fear, the smith approached the bright threshold steadily. He stuck the dirk in the doorway to keep it open and entered. Protected by the bible he carried on his breast, the fairies could not touch him; but they asked him, with a good deal of displeasure, what he wanted there.[21]

He answered: "I want my son, who I see down there, and I will not

---

[21] Today's popular culture has painted fairies as sweet, pretty, little creatures who can offer an adorably helpful sprinkle of magic whenever good folk need it. However, in previous centuries they were commonly regarded as evil. In *The Secret Commonwealth of Elves, Fauns and Fairies* (1682 first publ. New York: Dover Publications, 2008), Robert Kirk argues that fairies are "of a middle nature betwixt man and angels, as were the daemons thought to be of old" (p. 47). More recently, Lady Jane Wilde in *Legends, Charms and Superstitions of Ireland* (1887 first publ. New York: Dover Publications, 2006) is adamant that "fairies are the fallen angels who were cast down by the Lord God out of heaven for their sinful pride…and the devil gives to these knowledge and power and sends them on earth where they work much evil" (p. 96).

[22] Cockerels had a good reputation for scaring off fairies. Traditional folklore proposed a variety of ways to protect you and your house from fairies, among them: keeping a cockerel to scare them off; hanging a horse shoe in a prominent place in your home; always having a four-leaf clover on your person; wearing amulets made of various herbs, especially rowan berries; ringing bells in well-known fairy hangouts; and, intriguingly, turning your clothing inside out when walking at night.

go without him."

Upon hearing this, the whole company before him gave a loud laugh, which wakened up the cock the smith carried dozing in his arms. The cock at once leaped up on his shoulders, clapped his wings lustily, and crowed loud and long.[22]

The fairies, incensed, seized the smith and his son, and flung them out of the hill, throwing the dirk after them. And in an instant, the opening in the hill slammed shut and all was dark.

For a year and a day, the boy never did a turn of work, and hardly ever spoke a word. At last, one day, sitting by his father and watching him finishing a sword he was making for some chief, which required a particularly high skill set, he suddenly exclaimed: "That is not the way to do it." And taking the tools from his father's hands he set to work himself in his place and soon fashioned a sword, the like of which was never seen in this country before.

From that day on, the young man worked constantly with his father and became the inventor of a peculiarly fine and well-tempered weapon. The making of this weapon kept the two smiths, father and son, in constant employment, spread their fame far and wide, and rewarded them handsomely. As they had done before these events took place, they were well disposed to live content with all the world and very happy in each other's company.

THE BARRA WIDOW'S SON

There was a poor widow in Barra, and she had a babe of a son, and Iain was his name.[23] She would often go to the strand[24] to gather shellfish to feed herself and her babe. When she was on the strand one day, what did she see but a vessel to the west of Barra? Three of those who were on board put out a boat, and they were not long coming on shore.

She went to the shore and she emptied the shellfish beside her. The master of the vessel put a question to her:

"What thing is that?" She said that the food she had was strand shellfish. "And what little fair lad is this?"

"A son of mine," she said.

"Give him to me and I will give you gold and silver, and he will get schooling and teaching, and he will be better off with me than to be here with you."

"I had rather suffer death than give the child away."

"You are silly. The child and you will be well off if you let him go with me." He argued his point for a long time. In the end, for the

---

[23] From Alexander MacNeill, tenant and fisherman, living at Tangual, Barra, in the mid-nineteenth century. He heard the story from his father, Roderick MacNeill, who would often recite it. Roderick MacNeill died around 1820 at the age of 80. He had heard the story in his youth when it was commonly told.

[24] While a beach is specifically a sandy or pebbly shore, a strand is a more general term that can refer to any stretch of coastline, regardless of its composition.

love of the money, she gave in and agreed that he could take the child.

He called to his fellow seafarers: "Come here, lads. Go on board; here is a key. Open a press[25] in the cabin, and bring me a box that you will find in it." They went away, did that, and returned.

He took the box and opened it, emptying its rich contents with a gush into her skirt. He did not count it and simply took the child with him.

She remained as she was, and when she saw the child going on board the ship she would have given all she ever saw just to have him back again. The captain sailed away and went to England. He gave schooling and teaching to the boy on the vessel until he was eighteen years old. He called the boy Iain Albanach at first; but later gave him the name of Iain Mac a Maighstir (John, the master's son), because he was master of the vessel.

The owner of the vessel had seven ships at sea, and seven shops on shore—each ship going to her own shop with her cargo. On one occasion it happened that the seven ships were all at home together. The owner took the seven skippers to his house,

"I am growing heavy and aged," said he. "You are the seven masters; I would choose none other than you. I am without a man of clan[26] though I am married. I know not to whom I will leave my goods, and I have a great share[27]; there was none I would rather give it to than

---

[25] A press generally refers to a storage space or cabinet specifically designed to store clothes or linens.
[26] In other words: I don't have a male heir to take over the leadership of the family (the clan).
[27] a great deal of wealth

you, but you are without clan as I am myself."

"I have a son eighteen years of age in the ship," said the skipper. "He has lived all his life at sea."

"That is wonderful for me to hear!" said the owner. "I never knew that."

"Many a thing might the like of me have, and not tell it to you, sir," said the captain.

"Go and bring him down here to me so that I may see him." He went off and brought his son to present him to the owner.

"Is this your son?" asked the owner.

"It is," said the skipper.

"Would you rather stay with me, or go with your father on the sea as you have done before? I would make you my heir forever."

"Well then, sir, it was ever at sea that I was raised," said Iain Mac a Maighstir, "and I never got much on shore from my youth; so, at sea I would rather be. But since you have expressed a desire to keep me, let me stay with you."

"I have seven shops on shore, and you must take a hand in running one of the shops. There are clerks at every one of the shops," said he. "Not one of them will hold a bad opinion of himself that he is not as good as I."

"If you insist that I take one, I will take the seventh one of them," replied Iain.

He took the seventh shop, and on his first day of work he made it known through the town that an item that cost one pound would be reduced to fifteen shillings; and, likewise, everything in the shop was to be discounted. The shop was empty before the ships arrived. The owner came into the shop and counted the money. He noted that the shop was empty.

"Is it not wonderful to reduce something that was a pound to fifteen shillings?"

"My Oide[28]," said Iain, fearing the owner was angry, "are you taking that ill? Do you not see that I would sell every item in the shop seven times before the other shops could sell it once?"

"With that in mind, you must take the rest of the shops in hand, and manage them in this manner." Iain took the rest in hand, and he was a master above all the other clerks. When the ships came in, the shops were empty. Then his master said:

"Would you rather be master over the shops or go with one of the seven ships? You will get your choice of the seven ships."

"It is at sea I was ever raised and I will take a ship, sir."

"Come, send to me the seven skippers," the owner commanded. The seven skippers came. "Now," said he to the six skippers that were going with Iain, "Iain is going with you, and you will set three ships before and three behind, and he will be in the middle. Unless you bring him back whole to me, there is nothing for it but to seize you and hang you."

---

[28] foster father (of Irish derivation)

"Well, then, my adopted father," said Iain, "that is not the best strategy. The ships are going together and a storm may come and drive us from each other; let each do as best he may." And so it was agreed.

The ships sailed. Iain had loaded a cargo of coal on his own ship. There came on them a great day of storm and they were driven from each other. Where did Iain sail but to Turkey? He took anchorage in Turkey at early morning, and he decided to go on shore to take a walk. On his walk, he saw two men working with iron flails and with their shirts off. What had they but a man's corpse!

"What are you doing to the corpse?"

"He was a Christian," one said. "We had eight merks[29] against him[30], and since he did not pay us while he was alive, we will take it out of his corpse with the flails."

"Well then, leave him with me and I will pay you the eight merks."

He paid them, picked up the corpse, and left them. He put mold[31] and earth on him and buried him. After this, he continued his walk to see more of the land of the Turk. He went on a bit further and what should he see there but a great crowd of men together? He went over to where they were. There was a gaping red-hot fire and a woman stripped between the fire and them.

"What are you doing here?" he asked them.

---

[29] The merk was an ancient Scottish silver coin. Originally, the same word as a money mark of silver, the merk was in circulation at the end of the 16th century and in the 17th century.
[30] That is, he owed a debt to us of eight merks.
[31] Presumably meaning "clay" which was known to preserve bodies.

"The Great Turk[32] captured two Christian women," they replied. "They were caught on the ocean. He had them for eight full years. This one was promising him that she would marry him every year. But when the time came each year to marry him, she would refuse. He ordered her and the woman that was with her to be burnt. One of them was burnt, and this one is as yet unburnt."

"I will give you a good lot of silver and gold if you leave her with me, and you may say to him that you burnt her," said Iain.

They looked at each other and then told him they could agree to that arrangement. He took the woman with him on board his ship and clothed her in cloth and linen.

"Now," said she, "you have saved my life for me; you must take care of yourself in this place. You must go now to yonder change house.[33] The man of the inn will put a question to you about what cargo you have. Say you have a cargo of coal. He will say that would be well worth selling in the place where you are. Say it is for sale and that is why you are here; ask what offer will he make for it. He will say that tomorrow at six o'clock there will be a wagon of gold going down, and a wagon of coal coming up, so that the ship might be kept in the same trim[34], until six o'clock on the next night. Say that you will accept that proposal.

---

[32] This may be a reference to the Great Turkish War (1683-1699) which was a series of conflicts between the Ottoman Empire and some European powers of the day. Although Britain was not involved in that war, the Spanish Empire certainly was (the enslaved young lady turns out to be a Spanish princess).
[33] a small inn or alehouse
[34] In this case, trim refers to the ideal level of the waterline on the hull of a ship. If a ship is in trim, it will sail faster and safer. The principle is that the weight of the gold will compensate exactly for the weight of the coal. Which, of course, would make it a most attractive deal for Iain.

"But unless you are watchful, they will come in the night when every man is asleep, with muskets and pistols. They will drag the ship aground. They will kill every man on board, and then they will take the gold with them."

Iain went to the man at the inn and agreed with him as she had taught him. The following morning, they started the job of putting down the gold and taking up the coal. The skipper had a man standing looking out to make sure that the vessel remained in trim. Just before Iain went onshore, he gave an order to the sailors that the woman would oversee the ship while he was away, and that they should obey her instructions. When the coal was out, and the ship was as heavy with the gold as she had been with the coal, the woman spoke to the sailors:

"Put up the sails," said she, "and draw the anchors. Put a rope on shore." They did that. Iain came on board and the ship sailed away through the night. They heard a shot, but they were long gone, and they were never caught.

They sailed until they reached England. Three ships had returned, and the three skippers were in prison until Iain should come back. Iain went up and found his adopted father. The gold was taken on shore, and the old man had two-thirds and Iain a third. He got chambers for the woman in a place where she would not be troubled.

"Are you thinking that you might set off again?" the woman asked Iain. "I am thinking that I know enough of the world to be of help to you. You went on your mission before. If you would be so good as to go now for my purposes…"

"I will do that," he replied.

"Come to that shop over there; take from it a coat, brigis[35], and a waistcoat," she said. "Try if you can to get a cargo of herring, and you will go with it to Spain. When the cargo is loaded, come where I am before you leave."

When the cargo had been loaded on board he went to find her.

"Have you got the cargo on board?"

"I have," said Iain.

"There is an outfit here, and the first Sunday after you have reached Spain you will put it on, and you will go to the church in it. Here is a whistle[36], and a ring, and a book. Let there be a horse and a servant with you. You shall put the ring on your finger; let the book be in your hand.

"You will see in the church three seats: two twisted chairs of gold, and a chair of silver. Take hold of the book and be reading it, and when the first man goes out of the church, you leave as well. Wait not for any man or woman alive who may call after you, unless the King or the Queen meets you."

He sailed until he reached Spain; he took anchorage and he went up to the change house.

He asked for a dinner to be prepared for him. The dinner was set on

---

[35] Breeches—once a standard article of formal clothing in the Western world. They covered the body from the waist down, with separate coverings for each leg, usually stopping just below the knee, though occasionally reaching to the ankles. They were superseded in the nineteenth century by trousers.

[36] In this case, the whistle would have been a musical instrument, rather like a short flute.

the board[37]. They went about to call him to come to dinner. A trencher[38] was set on the board, and a cover on it, and the housewife said to him:

"There is meat and drink enough on the board before you, take enough, but do not lift the cover that is on top of the trencher."

She drew the door as she left. He began his dinner. He wondered what was under the trencher, imagining it may be full of gold or perhaps full of "daoimean."[39] Nothing had ever gone on a board before that he might not look at. He lifted the cover of the trencher, and what was on the trencher but a couple of herrings.

"If this is the thing she was hiding from me, she need not have bothered," he said to himself, and he ate one herring and one side of the other.

When the housewife saw that the herrings were eaten, she cried:

"Mo chreach mhor! My great ruin. What a disaster! There was never a day that I let down the great people of the realm until today!"

"What has befallen you?" said Iain.

"There never was a day that I might not put a herring before them until today."

"What would you give for a barrel of herrings?"

---

[37] The difference between a table and a board is that a board is simply a plank (or planks), sometimes polished, that rested on trestles and was used for eating meals. Tables, of course, have a surface that is fixed to legs.
[38] a wooden plate
[39] diamonds

"Twenty Saxon pounds," she replied.

"What would you give for a shipload?"

"That is a thing that I could not buy."

"Well, then, I will give you two hundred herrings for the two herrings, and I wish my ship were away and the herrings sold."

On the first Sunday, he bought a horse with a bridle and saddle, and hired a gillie. He went to the church; he saw the three chairs. The queen sat on the right hand of the king, and he sat on the left; he took the book out of his pocket and began reading.

It was not the sermon that accounted for the king's sad looks nor the queen's tears of sorrow. When the sermon ended, Iain followed the first man out the door.

There came three nobles running after him, shouting that the king had a matter for him. He would not return but merely took himself to the change house that night. He remained as he was until the next Sunday, and he went to the sermon; he would not stay for anyone, and he returned to the change house. On the third Sunday, he again went to the church. In the middle of the sermon the king and queen came out; they stood at each side of the bridle reins.

When the king saw him coming out, he let go of the rein; he took his hat off to the ground, and he made manners at him.

"By your leave, you needn't make such manners at me," said Iain. "It is I who should make them to yourself."

"If it were your will, I would be pleased if you would go with me to the palace to take dinner," said the king.

"Ud! Ud! It is a man below you with whom I should go to dinner."

They reached the palace. Food was set in the place of eating, drink in the place of drinking, music in the place of hearing. They were plying the feast and the company with joy and gladness because they had hopes that they would get news of their daughter.

"O, skipper of the ship," said the queen, hide not from me a thing that I am going to ask you.

"Anything that I know I will not hide from you," Iain replied

"And hide not from me that a woman's hand set that dress about your back, your coat, your brigis, and your waistcoat, and gave you the ring about your finger, and the book that was in your hand, and the whistle that you were playing."

"I will not hide it. With a woman's right hand every whit[40] of them was afforded to me."

"And where did you find her? I mean, the daughter of mine that is there."

"I know not to whom she is daughter. I found her in Turkey about to be burned in a great gaping fire."

"Did you see a woman along with her?"

---

[40] part or bit

"I did not see her; she was burned before I arrived. I bought her with gold and silver and took her with me. I have put her in a chamber in England."

"The king had a great General," said the queen, "and what should he do but fall in love with her? Her father was asking her to marry him, and she would not marry him. She went away on a vessel with the daughter of her father's brother, in the hope he would forget her. They went over to Turkey; the Turks caught them, and we had no hope of seeing her alive ever again.

"If it be your pleasure, and if you are willing, I will ready a ship to seek her," said the king. "If you marry her, you will have half the realm so long as the king lives, and the whole realm when he is dead."

"I scorn to do that," said Iain. "But send a ship and a skipper away, and I will take her home; and if that is her own will, perhaps I will not be against it."

A ship was made ready. But what should the General do but pay a lad to have him taken on board unknown to the skipper? The General got himself hidden in a barrel. They sailed off and, within a short time, they reached England. They took the young woman on board, and they sailed back for Spain. In the middle of the sea, on a fine day, he and she came up on deck, and what should he see but an island beyond him? The sea was very calm at the time.

"Lads, take me to the island for a while to hunt, until there comes on us the likeness of a breeze," said Iain.

"We will." They set him on shore on the island, left him there, and returned to the boat.

When the General saw that he was on the island, he promised more wages to the skipper and the crew, if they would leave him there; they agreed and left Iain on the island.

When she perceived that they had left Iain on the island, the woman went mad, and they were forced to bind her. They sailed on to Spain. They sent word to the king that his daughter had suddenly gone mad, as it seemed, for the loss of her husband and lover. The king betook[41] himself to sorrow, to black melancholy, and to woe and heart-breaking because of what had arisen. She was the only son or daughter he had.

Iain remained on the island, his hair and beard grown all over him. The hair of his head was down between his two shoulders; his shoes were worn to pulp; and he was without a thread of clothes that had not gone to rags. And he was without a bite of flesh on him, his bones merely sticking together.

On a night of nights, what should he hear but the rowing of a boat coming to the island?

"Are you there, Iain Albanach?" said the man in the boat. Though he was, he did not answer. He would rather find death at the side of a hill than be killed here by a stranger.

"I know that you hear me, and answer; it is just as well for you to answer me, else I will go up and take you down by force." Iain made himself known. "Are you willing to leave the island?"

"Well, then, yes I am," said Iain. "If someone were willing to take me."

---

[41] resorted to, or had recourse to

"What would you give to a man that would take you out of this?"

"There was a time when I might give something to a man who would take me out of this, but today I have not a thing."

"Would you give one-half of your wife to a man that would take you out of this?"

"I have not that," Iain replied.

"I do not say you have a wife; just *would* you give her away if you did."

"I would give her away."

"Would you give half your children to a man that would take you out of this?"

"I would give them."

"Come down here; sit in the stern of the boat." He sat in the stern of the boat. "Where would you rather go— to England or Spain?"

"To Spain." He went with him and, within a day, he was in Spain.

He went up to the change house; the housewife knew him in a moment. "Is this Iain!" said she.

"It is the sheath of all that there was of him that is here," he replied.

"Poorly has it befallen you!" said she. She went and sent a message to a barber's booth, and Iain was cleansed; and word to a tailor's booth, and clothes were made for him. She sent word to a shoemaker's booth, and shoes were brought to him.

On the following day, when he was properly cleansed and arrayed, he went to the palace of the king and played the whistle. When the king's daughter heard the whistle she gave a spring, and she broke the third part of the cord that bound her. They asked her to keep still, and they tied more cords on her.

On the next day, he gave a blast on the whistle, and she broke two parts of all that were on her. On the third day, when she heard his whistle, she broke three quarters; on the fourth day, she broke every cord that bound her.

She rose and she went out to meet him, and there never was a woman saner than she. Word was sent up to the King of Spain that she was not mad; and that the bodily presence of her husband and lover had come to her.

A coach was sent to fetch Iain; the king and his great courtiers were with him; he was raised up in celebration. Meat was set in the place of eating, drink in the place of drinking, music in the place for hearing; a cheery, hearty, jolly wedding was made. Iain got one-half of the realm; after the king's death, he received the realm in its entirety. The General was seized; he was torn among horses[42] and his remains burned to ashes, which were cast into the wind.

After the death of the king and queen, Iain was king over Spain. Three sons were born to him. One night he heard a knocking at the door.

---

[42] This was a medieval form of execution for serious crimes, such as killing a king. The victim's four limbs were attached by ropes to four horses, which were then set off on a gallop in different directions.

"The asker is come," said a voice. Who was there but the very man who rescued him off the island?

"Are you for keeping your promise?" said the one who came.

"I am," said Iain.

"Your own be your realm, and your children—and my blessing!" said the man. "Do you remember when you did pay eight merks for the corpse of a man in Turkey? That was my body. Health be yours! You will see me no more."

THE RIDIRE OF GRIANAIG AND IAIN THE SOLDIER'S SON

The Knight of Grianaig had three daughters, of such beauty that their like was not to be found or to be seen in any place.[43] There came a beast from the ocean and she took the daughters with her, and no one knew which way they had been taken, nor where they might be sought.

There was a soldier in the town and he had three sons. At the time of Christmas, the three boys were playing at shinny.[44] The youngest suggested that they should go and drive a hale[45] on the lawn of the Knight of Grianaig. The rest said that they should not go; that the knight would not be pleased; and that they would be bringing the loss of his daughters to his mind, laying sorrow upon him.

"Let that be as it pleases," said Iain, the youngest son, "but we will go there and we will drive a hale. I could not care less about the Knight of Grianaig; let him be well pleased or angry."

They went to play shinny, and Iain won three hales from his brethren. The knight put his head out of a window and saw them playing. He was extremely angry that anyone had the heart to play shinny on his

---

[43] The tale was recounted to Hector MacLean by Donald MacNiven, a lame carrier from Bowmore, Islay, on July 5, 1859. MacNiven heard the story many years before from an old man by the name of Neil MacArthur. The term "Ridire" signifies a knight or minor king. Grianaig is a Gaelic name (meaning sunny knoll) that has since been corrupted into Greenock

[44] The game is a variation of hockey played mostly by children with a curved stick and a ball or block of wood. The game is now more widely known as shinty, but in parts of Scotland it is still referred to as shinny.

[45] play a game of shinny

lawn—a thing that was bringing the loss of his three daughters to his mind, and laying contempt upon him.

He said to his wife: "Who is so impudent as to be playing shinny on my ground, and bringing the loss of my children to my mind? Let them be brought here in an instant so that punishment may be done upon them." The three strong lads were brought into the presence of the knight.

"What made you," said the knight, "go and play shinny upon my ground and bring the loss of my children to my mind? You must suffer pain for it."

"A preferable solution would be this," said Iain. "Since we have wronged you, it is better to build us a ship and we will go to seek your daughters, and whether they are under the leeward, or the windward, or under the four brown boundaries of the deep, we will find them before the end of a day and year. And we will bring them back to Grianaig."

"Though you are the youngest, it is in your head that the best counsel is to be found. The ship will be built for you," said the knight.

Wrights[46] were hired and a ship was made in seven days.[47] They put in as much meat and drink as they might need for the journey. The three soldier's sons faced her front to sea and her stern to land, and they went on their way.

<u>In seven days, they reached</u> a white sandy strand. When they went

---

[46] shipbuilders

[47] A remarkable build time but, then again, this is a folk tale. Late eighteenth-century shipbuilding records suggest that steaming and shaping the required timber alone could take up to two years.

on shore there were sixteen men at work, blasting the face of a huge rock, with a foreman watching over them.

"What place is this?" asked the skipper.

"Here is the place where the daughters of the Knight of Grianaig are to be married to three giants," said the foreman.

"By what means can we find where they are?"

"There are no means except to go up the face of this rock in this creel[48]."

The eldest son went into the creel, and when he was halfway up the rock, there came a stumpy black raven. The raven attacked him with its claws and his wings until he almost left him blind and deaf. The eldest son had no choice but to turn back.

The second son climbed into the creel, and when he was halfway up, the stumpy black raven returned. The bird set upon him and he, too, had no choice but to turn back as did the first son.

At last, Iain went into the creel. When he was up halfway the stumpy black raven launched a fierce attack on him, battering him about the face.

"Up with me quickly," shouted the third son, "before I am blinded here!"

He was pulled up the face of the rock. When he reached the top, the

---

[48] A large wicker basket, usually for holding fish. In this case, the use of a stout block and tackle has turned it into a mode of transport.

raven came to where he was and the bird said to him.

"Will you give me a quid of tobacco?"[49]

"You high-priced rogue! Little claim have you on me for giving that to you."

"Never you mind that, I will be a good friend to you. Now, you will go to the house of the big giant, and you will see the knight's daughter sewing, and her thimble will be wet with tears. If you need help, call upon me and I shall come."

Iain went on ahead until he reached the house of the giant. When he entered, the knight's daughter was at the same time sewing and crying.

"What brought you here?" said she.

"What brought you here?" he responded.

"I was brought here against my wishes."

"Yes, I know that. Where is the giant?"

"He is on the hunting hill."

"How can we get him home?" he asked.

"Shake the battle chain outside. But there is no one in the leeward, or in the windward, or in the four brown boundaries of the deep, who

---

[49] A common expression for a portion of tobacco. Quid is a corruption of "cud"—because it was used for chewing. The matter is further confused because quid has since become British slang for a one pound note (now a one pound coin).

will hold battle against the giant, except for young Iain the soldier's son from Albainn, and he is but sixteen years of age. He is still too young to go into battle against the giant."

Iain said nothing and went outside. He pulled at the chain but to no effect, and he was brought fully to his knees with the effort. He stood up again and shook the chain once more—and this time he broke a link in it. The giant heard it on the hunting hill.

"Aha!" said the giant, "who could move my battle chain but young Iain, the soldier's son from Albainn, and he is but sixteen years of age. Surely, he is too young yet?"

The giant put the game he had killed on a withy, and home he came.

"Are you young Iain, the soldier's son from Albainn?" he demanded.

"Not I," said Iain.

"Who, then, are you in the leeward, or in the windward, or in the four brown boundaries of the deep, that could move my battle-chain, if you are not young Iain the soldier's son from Albainn?"

"There is many a one in Albainn as strong as young Iain the soldier's son."

"No, no—not true. I know this from the prophecies."

"Never mind what you know in the prophecies," Iain retorted.

"In what way can you prove yourself?" said the giant.

"When I and my mother fell out with each other, and I wanted to get my way, it was in a tight wrestling match that we proved ourselves.

One time she would get the better of me, and two times she would not."

Immediately, the giant and Iain seized each other, and they grappled hard—until the giant finally brought Iain to his knees.

"I see," said Iain, "that you are the stronger."

"It is known that I am," said the giant.

They tackled each other again. They were twisting and hauling each other about. Iain struck the giant's ankle with his foot and brought him to the ground where he pounced on him, using every muscle to hold him down. He called upon the raven to help attack the giant.

The stumpy black raven quickly appeared and set upon the giant about the face and the ears with his claws and with his wings until he blinded him and deafened him.

"Have you got a sharp weapon that will take the head off this monster?" the raven asked.

"I have not," replied Iain.

"Put your hand under my right wing, and you will find a small sharp knife which I have for gathering briar-buds. Take the giant's head off with it."

He put his hand under the raven's right wing and he found the knife, and straight away he took the head off the giant.

"Now, Iain, you must go and find the eldest daughter of the Knight of Grianaig, and she will ask you to return her to her father and not to go any further. Do not listen to her. Carry on and find the middle daughter. And, of course, you shall give me a quid of tobacco."

"I will give that to you indeed; well have you earned it. You shall have half of all I have."

"I will not. There is many a long day to Bealtain."[50]

"I won't be here until Bealtain."

"Ah," said the raven. "You have knowledge of what has passed, but you have no knowledge of what is before you. Get warm water, and clean yourself up. You will find a vessel of balsam above the door. Rub it in your skin and go to bed, and you will be whole and wholesome tomorrow. And in the morning, you will go on to the house of the next giant."

He went in and he did as the raven asked him. He went to bed that night, and he was whole and wholesome in the morning when he arose.

"It is better for you," said the knight's eldest daughter in the morning, "not to go further, and not to put yourself in more danger. There is plenty of gold and silver here, and we will take it with us and return home."

"I will not do that," said he. "I will take the road ahead of me."

He went forward until he came to the house where the middle daughter of the Knight of Grianaig was being held. He went in and

---

[50] Bealtain is the Gaelic May Day festival, marking the beginning of summer. It is traditionally held on 1 May, or about midway between the spring equinox and summer solstice. This is the raven's way of saying to Iain that there is still a lot of work to be done before you start promising me things.

she was seated sewing and weeping, and her thimble was wet with her tears.

"What brought you here?" she asked.

"What brought you here?"

"I was brought here against my wishes," she replied.

"I have knowledge of that. What set you weeping?"

"I have but one night until I must be married to the giant," she sobbed.

"Where is the giant?"

"He is on the hunting hill."

"How can we get him home?" Iain asked.

"Shake the battle chain outside. But there is no one in the leeward, or in the windward, or in the four brown boundaries of the deep, who will hold battle against the giant, except for young Iain, the soldier's son from Albainn, and he is but sixteen years of age. He is still too young to go to battle against the giant."

Iain went outside and he gave a mighty haul at the chain, and he landed on both knees. He climbed back onto his feet and gave another haul at the chain, and this time he broke three links in it.

The giant heard that on the hunting hill.

"Aha!" said he, "Who could move my battle chain but young Iain, the soldier's son from Albainn, and he is but sixteen years of age. Surely, he is too young yet?"

The giant put the game he had killed on a withy, and home he came.

"Are you young Iain, the soldier's son from Albainn?"

"Not I," said Iain.

"Who, then, are you in the leeward, or in the windward, or in the four brown boundaries of the deep, that could move my battle-chain, if you are not young Iain the soldier's son, from Albainn?"

"There is many a one in Albainn as strong as young Iain the soldier's son."

"No, no, no—I know this from the prophecies," the giant replied.

"Never you mind what you know in the prophecies."

"In what way can you prove yourself?"

"In hard hugs of wrestling."

They seized each other and the giant wrestled him to his knees.

"Yours is my life," said Iain, "you are stronger than I. Let us try another turn."

They tried each other again, and Iain struck his heel on the giant's ankle and sent him flying so that he landed hard on the muscles of his back on the ground.

"Raven," said Iain, "a flapping of your wings would be a good thing now!"

The raven came and he blinded and deafened the giant, giving him a battering with his beak, with his claws, and with his wings.

"Do you have a sharp weapon?" the raven asked.

"I have not."

"Put your hand under my right wing, and you will find there a small sharp knife that I have for gathering briar buds. Take the giant's head off with it."

He put his hand under the root of the raven's right wing, and he found the knife and took the head off the giant.

"Now you shall go in and clean yourself with warm water, you will find a vessel of balsam. Rub it on yourself and go to bed, and you will be whole and wholesome tomorrow. This middle daughter will be certainly more cunning and more demanding than was the one before, asking you to return and not to go further. But pay no attention to her. And you shall give me a quid of tobacco."

"I will give it indeed; you are worthy of it."

He went in and he did as the raven asked him. When he got up the following morning, he was whole and wholesome.

"You would be wise," said the knight's middle daughter, "to return, and not put yourself in more danger; there is plenty of gold and silver here."

"I will not do that; I will go forward." She tried to argue with him but he would not relent.

He went forward until he came to the house in which the youngest daughter of the knight was being held. He went in and he saw her sewing, and her thimble wet with tears.

"What brought you here?"

"What brought you here?"

"I was brought here against my wishes," she wept.

"I know that."

"Are you young Iain the soldier's son from Albainn?"

"I am. What is the reason that you are weeping?"

"I have but this night of delay before I must marry the giant."

"Where is he?"

"He is on the hunting hill."

"How can I bring him home?"

"Shake the battle chain outside."

He went outside, and he gave a shake to the chain and it knocked him down on his backside.

He stood up again and gave it another shake, and this time he broke four links in it, and it made a great rattling noise. The giant heard that on the hunting hill; he put his withy of game on his shoulder.

"Who in the leeward, or in the windward, or in the four brown boundaries of the deep, could shake my battle chain but young Iain the soldier's son from Albainn? And if it is he, my two brothers are already dead."

He came home in his might, making the earth tremble before him and behind him.

"Are you young Iain the soldier's son?" he demanded.

"Not I."

"Who, then, are you in the leeward, or in the windward, or in the four brown boundaries of the deep, that could move my battle chain, if you are not young Iain the soldier's son from Albainn?"

"There is many a one in Albainn as strong as young Iain the soldier's son."

"Not true—I know this from the prophecies."

"I care not what is in your prophecies."

"In what way would you like your trial?"

"Tight wrestling ties."

They seized each other and the giant set him on his haunches.

"Let me go; yours is my life."

They caught each other again. Iain struck his heel on the giant's ankle, and the giant fell to the ground, landing hard on the top of his shoulder and the muscles of his back on the ground.

"Stumpy black raven, if only you were here now!" Ian wished.

No sooner said he the word than the raven came. He battered the giant about the face, and the eyes, and the ears, with his beak, and with his claws, and with his wings.

"Do you have a sharp weapon?"

"I have not," Iain lamented.

"Put your hand under the root of my right wing and you will find a small sharp knife that I have for gathering whortle berries. Use it to take his head off."

He did exactly that.

"Now," said the raven, "take a rest as you did last night, and when you return with the three daughters of the knight to the edge of the rock, you will go down first yourself, and they will go down after you. Remember: you go first and they come after you. And you shall give me a quid of tobacco."

"I will give it; you have well deserved it. Here it is—all I have."

"I will only take a quid; there is many a long day to Bealtain."

"I will not be here until Bealtain."

"You have knowledge of what is behind you, but you have no knowledge of what is before you," said the raven.

On the morrow they prepared asses, and on their backs they put the giants' gold and the silver. Iain and the three daughters of the knight reached the edge of the rock. For fear the daughters would become giddy, he sent them down with the asses, one after one in the creel. There were three caps of gold on the daughters, all finely decorated with diamonds in Roimh[51] and of such quality that their like was not to be found in the universe. He kept the cap of the youngest.

He waited and waited for the creel to be sent back, but it did not return. He would be waiting still for that creel to come up to fetch him. Despite the protests of the youngest daughter, the cunning older daughters insisted that they should abandon Iain and board the ship with the treasure. Away they went, back to Grianaig.

Iain was left atop the rock, and without any means to get out of the place. The raven came where he was.

"You did not take my counsel?"

"I did not take it. If I had taken it, I should not be as I am."

"There is no help for it, Iain. The one who will not take counsel must therefore take combat. That is the consequence. You shall give me a quid of tobacco."

"I will give it."

"You shall return to the giant's house, and you shall stay there tonight."

"Will you not stay with me yourself to keep me company?"

"I will not stay: it is not suitable for me."

---

[51] Rome

In the morning the raven returned, saying: "You shall now go to the giant's stable, and if you are quick and active, there is a steed there. Sea or shore are all one to her, and she may get you out of these straits."

They went together to the stable—a stable of stone, dug into a rock with a door of stone. The door was slamming without ceasing, backwards and forwards, from early day to night, and from night to day.

"You must now watch and be careful," said the raven. "Wait for the right moment and dart through the opening without the door slamming on you."

"You had best try first since you are better acquainted with this situation than me," said Iain.

"Fair enough."

The raven gave a bob and a hop and in he went, but the door took a feather out of the root of his wing, and he screeched.

"Poor Iain, if you could get in with as little pain as I, you would not complain."

Iain took a run back and a run forward, and then he took a spring to go in. The door caught him in its jaws and it sliced off half his buttocks. Iain cried out in agony, and then he fell cold dead on the floor of the stable.

The raven lifted him and carried him on the points of his wings out of the stable and to the giant's house. He laid him on a board face down. He went out and he gathered various medicinal plants, and he made ointments that he put upon him. In ten days Iain was as alive and well as ever he was.

He went out to take a walk and the raven went with him.

"Now, Iain, you must take my counsel. You will take no notice of anything unusual that you may see about the island. Nothing—got it?"

"Got it," replied Iain.

And you shall give me a quid of tobacco."

"That I shall do."

He was walking about the island, and going through a glen when he saw three full heroes[52]. They were stretched on their backs, with a spear upon the breast of each of them, and all were in lasting sound sleep and drenched in a bath of sweat.

"It seems to me that this is pitiable. What harm is there to lift the spears off them?" said Iain to himself.

He went and he removed the spears from them. The heroes awoke

---

[52] Full heroes were knights of the second highest order of warriors. The ancient rankings of warriors are described in the original version of "The Story of Conall Guilbeanach," as follows: "The dun was guarded by nine ranks of soldiers. There were nine warriors (CURAIDHNEAN) at the back of the soldiers that were as mighty as the nine ranks of soldiers. There were behind the warriors six heroes (GASGAICH) that were as mighty as the nine warriors and the nine ranks of soldiers. There were behind these six heroes three full heroes (LAN GASGAICH) that were as mighty as all that were outside of them; and there was one great man behind these three, that was as mighty as the whole of the people that there were altogether…"

instantly and stood up.

Said one of the knights: "Witness fortune and men, that you are young Iain the soldier's son from Albainn. It is demanded of you, as if spells and prayers have been cast upon you, that you must go with us through the southern end of this island, past the dark cave of the evil black fisherman."

He went away with the three full heroes. They saw a slender wisp of smoke coming out of a cave. They went to the outside of the cave.

One of the heroes went in and saw a hag there seated, and the tooth that was the last in her mouth would readily make a knitting pin in her lap, a staff in her hand, or a stirring stick for the embers. There was a turn of her nails about her elbows and a twist of her hoary hair about her toes. She was not joyous to look upon.

She seized a magic club and struck him on the head with it, turning him into a bare crag of stone. The others who were waiting outside wondered why it was taking so long for him to return.

"Go in," said Iain to another one, "and see what is keeping your comrade."

He went in and the carlin[53] did to him as she did to the other. The third went in, and she did to him as she did to the rest.

Iain went in last. There was a great red-skulled cat there, and she scattered a barrow full of red ashes about her fur to blind and confuse him. He struck her with the point of his foot and drove the brain out of her. He turned to the carlin.

---

[53] witch

"Don't do anything, Iain!" she cautioned him. "These men are under spells, and to put the spells off them you must go to the island of big women and collect a bottle of the living water from there. When you rub it on them, the spells will go and they will come alive." Iain turned back in a state of black melancholy.

"You did not take my counsel," said the raven, "and you have brought more trouble upon yourself.

"You shall go to lie down this night, and when you rise tomorrow you shall take with you the steed, and you shall give her food and water. Sea or land is all one to her, and when you reach the island of big women, sixteen stable lads will meet you. They will all be for feeding the steed, and for stabling her in for you. But do not let them. Say that you will yourself give her food and water.

"When you leave her in the stable, every one of the sixteen will put a key in the lock of the door and turn it once, but you will turn the key in the opposite direction for every turn that they put in. And you shall give me a quid of tobacco."

"I will indeed."

He went to rest that night and, in the morning, he saddled the steed and went on his way. He faced the steed's front to the sea and her back to the shore, and she strode in her might until they reached the island of big women. When he went on shore sixteen stable lads met him and every one of them asked to stable her and feed her.

"I will stable her and I will take care of her. I will not give her to anyone." He put her in the stable, and when he came out every man put a turn in the key and he put a turn against every turn that they put into it.

The steed spoke to Iain and warned him that they would be offering him every sort of drink, but that he should not take any drink from them except whey and water. The steed also warned him that he should take care and not sleep, and take his chance to escape.

He went in and every sort of drink was being put round about there, and they were offering each kind to him, but he would not take a drop of any drink except whey and water. They were drinking, and drinking until they fell asleep, stretched about the board[54].

When he came out from the chamber, he heard the very sweetest music that ever was heard. He went on and he heard in another place music much sweeter. He came to the side of a stair and he heard music sweeter and sweeter yet than he had heard before. And he fell asleep.

The steed broke out of the stable and came to where he was. She kicked him and woke him.

"You did not take my counsel," said she, "and there is no knowing now if you can achieve your task or not. "

Iain was filled with sorrow. He went into one of the chambers and there in a corner he saw a Sword of Light.[55] He seized the Sword of Light and took the sixteen beads[56] that were with it. When he reached the well, he filled a bottle and returned. The steed met him,

---

[54] A board is simply a plank or planks, sometimes polished, that rested on trestles and was used for eating meals.
[55] A Sword of Light appears also in "The Young King of Easaidh Ruadh," which is the first story in this anthology. In the current story, its appearance is rather fortuitous. Generally, the sword is positioned as part of a quest. The hero must obtain it to win the woman he loves and/or to break some kind of magical spell.
[56] It is not clear how these beads related to the sword, if at all.

and he set her front to sea and her back to shore, and he returned to the other island where the raven was waiting for him.

"You shall go and stable the steed," said the raven, "and then you will lie down for the night. In the morning you will go and bring the heroes back to life, and you shall slay the carlin. And do not be as foolish tomorrow as you were before now."

"Will you not come with me tonight to drive my dullness from me?"

"I will not come; it will not answer a need for me."

In the morning, he reached the cave.

"A hearty welcome! All hail to you, Iain," said the carlin.

"Greetings and ill-health to you," he replied

He shook the water on the men and they rose alive, and then he struck the carlin with his palm and scattered the brains out of her. Ian and the three knights then left and went to the southern end of the island. They saw the black fisherman there working at his tricks. Iain drew his palm and he struck him, scattering the brains out of him. He took the heroes home to the southern end of the island. The raven came to where he was waiting.

"Now, you shall go home, and you shall take with you the steed to which sea and shore are alike. The three daughters of the knight are to have a wedding, two to be married to your two brothers, and the other to the chief who was supervising the men at the face of the rock. You shall leave the cap with me. You only have to think of me when you need the cap, and I will be with you.

"If anyone asks you from where you have come, say that you have come from behind you; and if he asks you where you are going, say that you are going before you."

He mounted upon the steed, and he faced her front to sea and her back to shore, and away they went. No stop nor stay was made until they reached the old church in Grianaig. There was a grass meadow, a well of water, and a bush of rushes. He got off the steed.

"Now," said the steed, "You will take a sword and cut the head off me."

"I will not cut it off indeed," replied Iain. "It would be sad for me to do it and it would be ungrateful of me."

"You must do it. In me, there is a young girl under spells and the spells will not be broken until the head is taken off me. I and the raven were once courting; he was a young lad and I was a young girl. The giants laid Draoidheachd[57] magic upon us, and they made a raven of him and a steed of me."

He drew his sword[58], turned his back, and took the head off her with a scutching[59] blow. He left the head and the carcass there. He continued forward and a carlin met him.

"From whence did you come?" said she.

---

[57] Druidic sorcery.
[58] No doubt, this is the Sword of Light that Iain stumbled across and appropriated earlier. There is no indication that this was the only sword that could be used to cut off the filly's head, since she refers only to "a sword."
[59] Scutching is a step in the dressing of flax or hemp in preparation for spinning. The scutching process separates the impurities from the raw material. The insinuation is that the blow was one of dismembering power.

"I am from behind me."

"Where are you going?

"I am going before me."

"That is the answer of a castle man."[60]

"An answer that is appropriate for an impudent carlin such as you are."

He went in with her and he asked for a drink, and he was given one.

"Where is your man?" asked Iain.

"He is at the house of the knight seeking gold and silver to make a cap for the knight's young daughter, such as her sisters have; and the like of which are not to be found in Albainn," said she

The smith came home. "What is your trade, lad?" he said.

"I am a smith."

"That is good, and I'd be glad if you could help me make a cap for the knight's young daughter, for she is going to marry tomorrow."

"But you know you cannot make that, don't you?" said Iain.

"It must be tried; unless I make it, I shall be hanged tomorrow," the smith sighed. "Here, you had best make it."

---

[60] The modern equivalent might be: "This is the answer of a politician."

"Lock me into the smithy workshop. Keep the gold and silver," Iain said, "and I will have the cap for you in the morning."

The smith locked him in. He called upon the raven to be with him. The raven came, broke in through the window, and the cap was with him.

"You shall take the head off me now," said the raven.

"It would be sorrowful for me to do that, and it would not be my thanks."

"You must do it. There is a young lad under spells in me, and the spells will not be cast off until my head comes off."

Iain drew his sword and he scutched the raven's head off, and that was not hard to do. In the morning the smith came in, and Iain gave him the cap. Iain then fell asleep. He was awoken by a noble-looking youth, with brown hair.

"I," said he, "am the raven, and the spells are off me now."

He walked down with him to where he had left the dead steed, and a young woman met them there, as lovely as eye ever saw.

"I," said she, "am the steed, and the spells are off me now."

The smith went with the cap to the house of the knight. The servant maid went to the knight's young daughter and presented her with the cap the smith had made. She looked at the cap.

"He never made that cap. Tell the lying rogue to bring hither the man who made him the cap or else he shall be hanged without delay."

The smith went and he brought the man who gave him the cap and, when she saw him, she was filled with joy. The whole matter was explained and cleared up. Iain and the knight's youngest daughter married, and backs were turned on the other sisters. They were driven away through the town with stick swords and straw shoulder belts.

THE STORY OF CONALL GUILBEANACH

Once upon a time, there was a young king in Eirinn, and when he came to man's estate the high counselors of the realm advised him to marry.[61] He was more inclined to go to foreign countries first to acquire more knowledge and be better instructed on how the realm should be regulated. He made arrangements for the running of Eirinn until he returned.

He went to Greece and remained there for a while until he had gained as much learning as he could in that realm. Then he left Greece and went to Italy to learn more. When he was in that country, he made acquaintance with the young King of Iubhar, and they were good comrades together; and when they had garnered all the experience they could in Italy, they thought of going home.

The young King of Iubhar invited the young King of Eirinn to visit the realm of Iubhar and to stay there for a while with him. The King of Eirinn agreed to accompany him, and they were together in the fortress of Iubhar for a while, enjoying sports and hunting.

---

[61] The title of the story in Campbell's 1860-62 anthology identifies the hero as Conall Gilban. The story itself repeatedly refers to him as Conall Guilbeanach. The Archives and Catalogue of the National Library of Scotland uses the title "The Tale of Conall Guilbeanach"—and that notation is therefore preferred here. This story comes from an extraordinary manuscript that fills some 60 foolscap pages (8.5"×13.5"). At a point in the 1850s, it was narrated by John MacNair, a shoemaker, who lived at Clachaid, Dunoon, and written down by John Dewar, a laborer who was working in the woods at Rosneath, a village on the western shore of Loch Gare. MacNair had been told the story many decades before by one Duncan Livingston, who lived in Glendaruel on the Cowal peninsula in Argyle and Bute.

The King of Iubhar had an exceedingly handsome sister; she was modest and gentle in her ways, and she was well educated. The young King of Eirinn fell in love with her, and she fell in love with him. He wanted to marry her, and she wanted to marry him, and the king of Iubhar was willing that the wedding should go ahead.

But the young King of Eirinn went home first, gathered together the high counselors of the realm, and told them what he desired to do. The high counselors of the realm of Eirinn advised their king to marry the sister of the King of Iubhar.

The King of Eirinn went back and married the king's sister, and the King of the Iubhar and the King of Eirinn made a league together. If straits, or hardships, or extremity, or anything counter should come upon either, the other was to go to his aid.

When they had settled each thing as it should be, the two kings gave each other a blessing and the King of Eirinn and his queen went home to Eirinn.

After little more than a year they had a young son, and they gave him Eoghan as a name. Good care was taken of him, as should be the case of a king's son. Just over a year later, they had another son and they gave him Claidheamh as his name. Care was taken of this one as had been taken of his brother. And a year after that they had another son, and they gave him Conall as a name, and as much care was taken of him as had been taken of the other two.

The boys were coming on well, and, at a fitting time, a teacher was employed for them. They learned as much as the teacher could give them.

One day, when the children were out at play, the king and queen were walking past and watching their children.

Said the queen: "This is well, and well enough, but more than this must be done for our children. I think that we ought to send them to the Gruagach[62] of Beinn Eibhinn[63] to learn skills and martial arts. There is not in the sixteen realms another man who is as expert in such matters as the Gruagach of Beinn Eibhinn."

The king agreed with her, and word was sent to the Gruagach. He came, and Eoghan and Claidheamh were sent with him to Beinn Eibhinn to learn the feats and skills, and whatever else besides, that the Gruagach could teach them.

The parents thought that Conall was too young to send him there at that time. When Eoghan and Claidheamh had been with the Gruagach for about a year, they came back with him for a visit to their father's house. They were sent back again, and the Gruagach continued teaching the king's children.

He took them with him one day up Beinn Eibhinn, and when they were around halfway up the mountain, the king's children saw a round brown stone, looking as if it was set aside from other stones.

They asked what was the reason for that stone being set aside from all the other stones on the mountain. The Gruagach said to them that the name of that stone was the Stone of the Heroes. Anyone who

---

[62] A Gruagach is a wizard-champion or wizard/druid—a hobgoblin with high acumen and some supernatural powers.
[63] Campbell records this as Beinn Eidinn but it is possible the reference is to Beinn Eibhinn (preferred here) which is remotely located as the most western peak along a rump of Highland mountains stretching between Alder and Laggan. Its summit ridge encircles the little lake named Lochan a'Charra Mhoir.

could lift that stone until he could place the wind between it and the earth was deemed a hero.

Eoghan went to try to lift the stone. He put his arms about it, and he lifted it to his knees. Claidheamh seized the stone, and he put the wind between it and the earth.

Said the Gruagach to them: "You are but young and tender. Don't injure yourselves by lifting things that are too heavy for you. Wait until the end of a year and you will be much stronger than you are now."

The Gruagach took them back to his home and taught them various feats and activities and, at the end of a year, he led them again up the mountain. Eoghan and Claidheamh went to the stone. Eoghan lifted it to his shoulders and set it down. Claidheamh lifted the stone to his lap. The Gruagach said to them: "There is neither lack of strength nor learning with you; I will return you to your father."

A few days after that, the Gruagach returned to the king's house and he gave the children to their father. He said that the king's sons were the strongest and the best taught that there were in the sixteen realms. The king gave thanks and rewards to the Gruagach, and he sent Conall with him.

The Gruagach began to teach Conall to do tricks and feats, and Conall pleased him well. One day he took Conall with him up the face of Beinn Eibhinn, and they reached the place where the round brown stone, known as the Stone of the Heroes, was to be found. Conall noticed it, and he asked as his brothers had done, and the Gruagach said as he said before.

Conall put his hands about the stone, and he put the wind between it and earth, and they went home. He remained with the Gruagach gaining more and more skills and knowledge.

The next year after that they again went up Beinn Eibhinn where the round brown stone was to be found. Conall thought that he would test if he was strong enough to lift the heroes' stone. He caught the stone, and he raised it on the top of his shoulder, and on the faggot gathering place of his back[64], and he carried it aloft to the top of Beinn Eibhinn, and down to the bottom of Beinn Eibhinn, and back up again, and he left it where he found it.

And the Gruagach said to him, "Ach! You have enough strength—now let's see if you have enough swiftness."

The Gruagach pointed out a blackthorn bush that was a short way from them, and he said, "If you can give me a blow with that blackthorn bush yonder before I reach the top of the mountain, I may have to give up instructing you." And the Gruagach immediately started running up the hill.

Conall sprang to the bush; he thought it would take too much time to cut it with his sword, so he simply pulled it out by the root and ran after the Gruagach. Before the Gruagach was even a short way up the mountain, Conall was at his back striking him at the back of his knees with the blackthorn bush.

The Gruagach said: "I will stop giving you instructions, and I will take you home to your father." But although the Gruagach wished to take Conall home, the boy was not willing to go until he had gained every shred of knowledge he could from the Gruagach. He stayed

---

[64] That is, he put it on his back across his shoulders, as would be done with bundles of sticks (faggots).

with him for another year and, after that, they returned to the king's home.

The king asked the Gruagach how Conall had taken to learning.

"It is certainly true," said the Gruagach, "that Conall is the young man who is the strongest and best taught in the sixteen realms—and, if he gets days[65], he will increase that heroism further."

The king gave full reward and thanks to the Gruagach for the care he had taken of his son. The Gruagach gave thanks to the king for the reward he had given him. They gave each other a blessing, and the Gruagach and the king's sons gave each other a blessing. The Gruagach returned home, fully pleased with how things had turned out.

All the sons of the King of Eirinn had completed their learning and they were with the king and queen in the fortress—they were full of rejoicing with music and celebration.

But suddenly, a messenger arrived from the King of Iubhar, reporting that the Turcaich[66] were at war with him and attempting to capture his land from him. His country was sorely overrun with Turks and they were numerous, powerful, and proud—and fiercely merciless, without kindness.

Some mysterious qualities about them were incomprehensible. Though they were slain one day, the next day they would be alive, coming forth to battle as fiercely as they ever were before. Though they were slain today they would be alive tomorrow.

---

[65] If he lives long enough—life was more arduous and precarious in those times.
[66] Turks

The messenger entreated the King of Eirinn to come to the aid of the King of Iubhar, in accordance with his words and his covenants. The King of Eirinn had to help the King of the Iubhar because of the heavy vows he had made: if strife, danger, straits, or any hardship should come against the one king, then the other king was to go to his aid.

They readied for departure, sending a ship with provisions and arms, and other ships loaded with everything else that they might require—noble ships indeed.

The King of Eirinn gave out an order that every man in the kingdom should assemble in readiness to go to the aid of Iubhar.

The King of Eirinn asked: "Is there any man fit to remain to keep safe the wives and sons of Eirinn until the King of Eirinn comes back? Oh, you, my eldest son, you must stay to keep the kingdom of Eirinn for your father, and your reward shall be the third part of the kingdom for life, and at his death."

"You seem light-minded to me, my father," said the eldest son, "when you utter such idle talk. I would rather have one day of battle and combat against the great Turk than the entire kingdom of Eirinn."

"There is no help for it," said the king. "You, my middle son, must stay to keep the kingdom of Eirinn for your father, and for this, you will have half the kingdom for his life and at his death."

"Do not speak, my father, of such a silly thing! What strong love should you have yourself for going, that I might not have?"

"There is no help for it," said the King of Eirinn.

"Oh, Conall," said the king, "you have ever earned my blessing and never deserved my curse. Stay you to keep safe the wives and sons of Eirinn for your father until he returns home again, and you shall have half the realm of Eirinn for yourself, for my life, and at my death."

"Well then, father, I will stay for your blessing, and not for the realm of Eirinn, however much I like that idea."

Conall and his father and his brothers gave a blessing to each other; and the King of Eirinn and his two sons, Eoghan and Claidheamh, went on board a ship, and they hoisted the speckled flapping sails up against the tall, tough masts.

Conall was heavy and downcast when his father and brothers left him, and he sat down on the shore and fell asleep. The rude awakening he received was that of a wave sweeping him out to sea and of another wave washing him back against the shore. Conall got up swiftly and was annoyed with himself for falling asleep. He said to himself:

"Is this the first exploit I have done? It is no wonder that some would say I am too young to take care of the realm since I cannot take care of myself."

There was not a man left in the realm of Eirinn but Conall, and few were left in the realm of Laidheann. The King of Laidheann and his forces had accompanied the King of Eirinn in the expedition to fight the Turks. The daughter of the King of Laidheann stayed behind in her father's castle with five hundred soldiers to guard her.

Anna Diucalas was her name. She was, as the saying goes, the very drop of woman's blood and the most beautiful woman who had ever stood on the leather of a cow or horse.

Conall became melancholy because he had to stay alone in the realm of Eirinn. He was a warrior without peer, and yet it was not he but the others who had been sent to war. He thought that there was nothing that would cure his sorrow better than a visit to the green mound he knew so well beside Beinn Eudainn[67].

This was a place his father knew and loved. The young King of Eirinn and the King of Laidheann were comrades, and fond of each other, and they used to go to the green mound on the side of Beinn Eudainn to seek pastime and pleasure of mind. Conall, too, had grown to love it.

When he reached the green mound, he laid his face downwards on the hillock, and he daydreamed that nothing would suit him better than to find his match of a woman. Then he gave a glance to the side and what should he see but a raven sitting on a heap of snow? And Conall got it into his head that he would not take a wife unless her hair was as black as the raven, her face as fair as the snow, and her cheeks as red as blood.

To his knowledge, only one such a woman was to be found—the woman that the King of Laidheann left in his castle; his daughter, Anna Diucalas. But getting to her would not be easy on account of the five hundred soldiers left to guard her. Nonetheless, he still thought that it might just be possible.

<u>He took this burden upon himself.</u> He boarded a skiff and rowed

---

[67] A mountain mentioned in a number of stories but of uncertain location.

until he came to the shore of Laidheann. He did not know the road, but he took instructions from every traveler and walker that he fell in with, and eventually, he came to a small strait. There was a ferry boat on the strait, but the boat was on the other side of the narrows.

He stood a little while looking at its breadth. At last, he put his palm on the point of the spear, and the shaft in the sea, and gave a rounded spring, and he was over![68]

He found himself on top of a high cliff. Looking down below, he saw the very finest castle that had ever been seen from the beginning of the universe to the end of eternity. There was a huge wall at the back of the fortress, and iron spikes within a foot of each other, all around. There was a man's head upon every spike except for one. Fear struck him, and he fell to shaking. He thought that this was a sign that his head would soon be decorating the headless spike.

The dun[69] was guarded by nine ranks of soldiers. There were nine warriors at the back of the soldiers who were as mighty as the nine ranks of soldiers. There were behind the warriors six heroes who were as mighty as the nine warriors and the nine ranks of soldiers. Behind these six heroes, three full heroes were as mighty as all that were outside of them. And there was one great man, behind these three, who was as mighty as the whole of the assembled host.

Many a man tried to capture Ann Iuchdaris but none of them was left alive.

Conall came to near to the soldiers, and asked permission to go in,

---

[68] This is a remarkable and valuable skill, used not only here but in other popular folk stories where it conveniently circumvents seemingly impossible obstacles.
[69] castle

saying he would bring no harm to the woman inside.

"I perceive," said one of them, "that you are a beggar who lived in the land of Eirinn. What honor would the King of Laidheann have if he should come back and find his daughter shamed by a coward of Eirinn?"

"I won't waste my time asking for directions from you," said Conall. He looked at the men who were guarding the dun, his head sweeping around with ears that were sharp to hear and eyes rolling to see. A glance that he gave aloft to the dun revealed an open window and a Breast of Light[70] on the inner side of the window combing her hair. Conall stood a little while gazing at her but, at last, he put his palm on the point of his spear, gave his rounded spring, and next thing he was in at the window beside Breast of Light.

"Who is this youth who has sprung so daringly in at the window to see me?" said she.

"Someone who has come to take you away," said Conall.

Breast of Light laughed, and she said: "Did you not see the soldiers who are guarding the dun?"

"I saw them," said he. "They let me in, and they will let me out."

She gave another laugh and said: "Many a one has tried to take me out from this place but none has done it yet. They all ran out of luck in the end. My counsel to you is that you should not try."

[70] George William Cox, *The Mythology of the Aryan Nations* (London: Kegan Paul, Trench & Company, 1882, p. 391), connects the term "Breast of Light" to ancient Hellenic Myth.

Conall put his hand about her waist and raised her in his oxter[71]. He took her out to the rank of soldiers. Then he put his palm on the point of his spear, gave his rounded spring, and leaped over their heads. He ran so swiftly that they could not see that it was Breast of Light he had, and when he was out of sight of the dun he set her on the ground. Breast of Light heaved a heavy sigh.

"What is the meaning of your sigh?" asked Conall.

"It is," said she, "that there came many a one to seek me who suffered death for my sake. And yet it is a coward of the great world who succeeded in taking me away."

"How do you make that out?" said Conall.

"Because there were so many men around the dun, fear would not allow you to tell the sorriest of them who it was who took away Breast of Light, nor tell them where you were taking her."[72]

Said Conall: "Give me your three royal words, and your three baptismal vows, that you will not move from this spot, and I will go back and tell them these things."

"I will do that," said she.

---

[71] armpit

[72] This seems a rather precious piece of fault finding. But, according to Campbell, it is in the spirit of the Icelandic code of honor, as expressed in the Njal Saga: "It was all fair to kill a man if it was done openly, or even unawares if the deed were not hidden, and here the lady was offended because the swain had not declared his name, and quite satisfied when he did." At this point, of course, Conall has not killed anyone but the irony is that, in satisfying his lady's requirement and returning to the castle's defenders to explain himself, he ends up slaying most of them.

Conall turned back to the dun, with nothing in the world in the way of arms to help him—except for a horse's jaw bone which he found in the road.

When he arrived at the dun, he asked them what they would do to a man who tried to take away Breast of Light.

"Simply this," said they. "We will cut off his head and set it on a spike."

Conall looked under them, over them, through and before them, for the one with the biggest knob and slenderest shanks. And, having surveyed them, he caught hold of the slenderest shanked and biggest knobbed man and with the head of that one he smashed the brains out of the rest.

Then he drew his sword, and he began on the nine warriors, and he slew them, and he killed the six heroes that were at their back, and the three full heroes who were behind these, and this then left only the big man. Conall struck him with a slap and drove his eye out on his cheek. He then flattened him and stripped his clothes off.

In short, Conall left no one to tell the tale of what happened or embellish news of bad doings except for this one big man who had been clipped like a bird or a fool. Even if he had ten tongues of a true wise bard in his head, the man would still only be trying to explain the humiliation and decimation of himself and his men—by a mere youth who had come to town and put the lot of them to the sword.

He asked the big man about the King of Laidheann, and the big man said that he was back from war and on the hunting hill with his court and his following retinue of men and beasts.

Said Conall to him: "I lay it on you as disgrace and contempt that you must go, stripped naked as you are, to tell the King of Laidheann that Conall Guilbeanach came, the son of the King of Eirinn, and that he has taken away his daughter Breast of Light.

When the big man understood that his life was to be spared, he ran in great leaps and in a rough trot, like a venomous snake or a deadly dragon. He would catch the swift March wind that was before him, but the swift March wind that was after him could not catch him.

The King of Laidheann saw him coming, and he said: "What evil has befallen the dun this day, when the big man is coming to us stark naked like this?" They sat down, and at last the man arrived.

Said the king: "Tell us your tale, big man."

"My lord, I have a tale of hate to tell you—that there came Conall Guilbeanach, son of the King of Eirinn, and slew all the men guarding the dun. It was not my might or my valor that rescued me. Rather, that he laid it on me as a disgrace and reproach that I should go naked to tell this story to my king—to tell him that there came Conall Guilbeanach, son of the King of Eirinn, and he has taken away Breast of Light, your daughter."

"Much good may it do him then," said the King of Laidheann. "If it is a hero like that who has taken her away, he will keep her better than I could keep her, and my anger will not go after her."[73]

Conall returned to the woman after he had annihilated the dun's host

---

[73] The king seems curiously relaxed about the slaying of his garrison and the abduction of his daughter. It may be that, as per Campbell's observation (see Note 72), Conall's courtesy in explaining his actions has assuaged the king's ire.

of defenders.

"Come now," said he to Breast of Light, daughter of the King of Laidheann, "and walk with me. If you had not spoken to me so spitefully, your father's men would still be alive and standing at their posts. And since you did speak in that spiteful way, you will now walk by yourself.[74] Let your foot be even with mine."[75]

She rose well-pleased, and she went away with him. They reached the narrows, boarded the ferry boat, and crossed the strait. Conall had neither steed, horse, nor harness, and so Breast of Light had to take to her feet. When they reached where Conall had left the currach[76] they put the boat on the brine and rowed over the ocean.

They came to land at the lower side of Bein Eudainn, in Eirinn. They left the boat and proceeded on their way to the green mound at the foot of Beinn Eudainn. Conall told Breast of Light that he had a curious failing—every time that he did any deed of valor he must sleep before he could do brave deeds again.

"There now, I will lay my head on your lap."

"You will not," she said, "for fear you should fall asleep."

"And if I do, will you not waken me?"

"What manner of waking is yours?"

"You should rock me greatly hither and thither, and if that will not

---

[74] as opposed to being carried
[75] keep up with me
[76] A small traditional Celtic boat with a wooden frame and a skin of hide or canvas.

rouse me, you will pinch the breadth of a penny piece of flesh and skin from the top of my head. If that will not wake me, you will seize that great slab of a stone over there, and you will strike me between the mouth and nose. And if that does not wake me, just leave me alone."[77]

He laid his head on her lap and, in an instant, he fell asleep.

He was not long asleep when she saw a great vessel sailing in the ocean. Each path was crooked and each road was level for her until she came to the green mound at the side of Beinn Eudainn.

There was only a single, huge man on the ship, and he managed the rudder in her stern, the cable in her prow, the tackle in her middle. Each loose rope he would tie, and each rope that was fast he would loosen.

He brought the ship to the foot of Beinn Nair and then leaped on shore. The big man then caught hold of the prow of the ship, and he hauled her whole nine lengths and nine breadths up upon green grass, where the force of foes could not move her without feet following behind them.[78]

He came where Breast of Light was, and where Conall was asleep with his head on her lap. He gazed at Breast of Light, and she said: "What are you looking for? Where are you going?"

---

[77] Donald A. MacKenzie, *Myths of Crete & Pre-Hellenic Europe* (London: The Gresham Publishing Company, 1917, p. 31) notes: "After or before great heroes performed deeds of valor, fighting against monsters or famous rivals, they fell into profound slumber. Heroines had to awaken them by cutting off a finger-joint, a part of an ear, or a portion of skin from the top of the head."
[78] without lots of people to help them

"Well, they were telling me that Breast of Light, daughter of the King of Laidheann, is the finest woman in the world, and I was going to seek her for myself."

"That is hard enough to get," said she. "She is in yonder castle, with five hundred soldiers for her guard that her father left there."

"Well," said he, "though she were brighter than the sun, and more lovely than the moon, past you I will not go."

"Well, you seem silly to think of taking me with you instead of that woman. I am not even worthy to go and untie her shoe."

"Be that as it may, you will go with me. I know that it is you by your beauty, Breast of Light, daughter of the King of Laidheann."

"That is wishful thinking," said she "I am not she, but a farmer's daughter and this is my brother; he lost his flock this day, and he was running after them backwards and forwards throughout Eudainn, and now he is tired and taking a nap."

"Be that as it may," said he, "there is a mirror in my ship, and the mirror will not rise[79] for any woman in the world, except for Breast of Light, daughter of the King of Laidheann. If the mirror rises for you, I will take you with me, and if it does not, I will leave you here."

He went for the mirror. Fear seized her, and she could not awaken

---

[79] Mythological stories around the world make use of mirrors (in the form of glass or reflective pools of water, or plates of copper, silver or bronze) in various ways: as revealers of truths and knowledge; as premonitions of bad luck if they break; as traps to ensnare souls; as prophets of things to come. The narrator leaves it to our imagination to determine what the huge man's mirror looks like when it rises.

Conall. The man looked in the mirror, and the mirror rose for her, and he went back to where she was.

Said the big one: "I will be certain of this matter before I go further." He plucked the sword of Conall from its sheath, and it was covered in blood.

"Ha!" said he, "I am right enough in my guess. Waken your champion, and we will test each other with swift wrestling, the might of hands, and hardness of blades, to see which of us has the best right to have you."

"Who are you?" said Breast of Light.

"I," said the big man, "am Mac-a-Moir MacRigh Sorcha, son of the mighty King of Light. It is in pursuit of you that I came."

"Will you not waken my companion?" said she.

He went, and he prodded him from his thumbs to the top of his head. "I cannot rouse the man. I like him as well asleep as awake."

Breast of Light got up and began to rock Conall hither and thither, but he would not wake up.

Said Mac-a-Moir: "Unless you wake him you must go with me and leave him in his sleep."

Said she: "Give you to me, before I go with you, your three royal words and your three baptismal vows that you will not seek me as a wife or as a sweetheart until the end of a day and a year after this, to give Conall time to come in my pursuit."

Mac-a-Moir gave his three royal words and his three baptismal vows[80] to Breast of Light, that she should be a maiden until the end of a day and a year, to allow time for Conall to come in pursuit of her if he dared to do so.

Breast of Light took the sword of Conall from the sheath, and she wrote on the sword what had happened. She took the ring from off the finger of Conall, put her ring on his finger in its place, and then put Conall's ring on her finger. She went away with Mac-a Moir, leaving Conall asleep.

The big man took the woman with him on his shoulder and he went to his ship. He shoved out the ship and he pointed her prow to sea, and her stern to shore. He hoisted the flapping white sails against the tall mast, and he left at great speed.

When Conall awoke on the green mound he found no one but himself, a shorn one and bare alone. He glanced around and saw the cattle herds that the King of Eirinn and Laidheann had left, dancing for joy on the points of their horns. He thought that they were mocking him for what had befallen him. He went to kill one with the other's head, and there was such a grim look upon him that the little herd fled out of his way.

He shouted at them: "Why are you fleeing from me, little herd of Beinn Eudainn, as if you are mad—are you mocking me for what

---

[80] The three royal words will differ from one royal family to the next. The British royal family has four words, adopted almost a thousand years ago: "Dieu et mon droit" (God and my right). The Dutch royal family has the motto "Je Maintiendrai" (I will maintain) used since the time of William of Orange in the seventeenth century. The three baptismal vows may be summarized as Renunciation, Faith, and Obedience: the renunciation of the Devil and all his works; belief in all the articles of the Christian faith; and obedience to the will of God.

has happened to me?"

"We are not," said they. "It was grievous for us to see how it befell you."

"What, my fine fellows, did you see happening to me?"

Replied the little herd: "You are likely to be madder than any one of us. If you had seen the rinsing, and the sifting, and the riddling[81] that they had at your expense at the foot of the hill, you would not have much esteem for yourself. I saw," said the little herd, "the one who was with you putting a ring on your finger."

Conall looked, and it was the ring of Breast of Light that was on his finger.

Said the little herd: "I saw her writing something on your sword, and putting it into the sheath."

Conall drew his sword, and he read: "There came Mac-a-Moir, the King of Sorcha, and took me away, Breast of Light; I am to be free for a year and a day in his house waiting for you if you have courage enough to come in pursuit of me."

Conall put his sword into its sheath, and he gave three royal words.

"I lay it on myself as spells and as crosses, that stopping by night and staying by day, is not for me until I find the woman. Where I take my supper, there I will not take my dinner. I swear also that

---

[81] "the rinsing, and the sifting, and the riddling…" Having taken umbrage at being called mad, the herd (which has assumed a kind of choric tenor in dealing with Conall) mischievously throws out an inane trill of words designed to rile Conall with its vague inference of untoward behavior on the part of his beloved.

there is no place I go where I will not leave the fruit of my hand there to boot. The children that are newly born shall hear of it, and those as yet unborn shall hear tell of it."

Said the little herd to him: "There came a ship to the shore down there. The sailors went to the hostelry, and if you are quick enough you may be away with their ship before they come back."

Conall left and went on board the ship, and he was out of sight with her before the mariners came back.

He gave her prow to sea, and her stern to shore, helm in her stern, rope in her prow, that each road was smooth, and crooked each path until he went into the realm of Lochlann at a place which was called the Battle of Bullets. But, in truth, he had no idea where he was.

He leaped on shore, and he seized the prow of the ship and pulled her up on dry land, her whole nine lengths and nine breadths, where the force of foes could not move her without feet following behind them.

The lads of the realm of Lochlann were playing shinny on a plain, with Gealbhan Greadhna, the son of the King of Lochlann, amongst them.

Conall stood singing iolla[82] to them, and the ball came to the side where he was. Conall kicked the ball, and he drove it out on the goal boundary against the Prince of Lochlann. The Prince came over to where he was, and he said:

"You, man, that came upon us from the ocean—it would be a small

---

[82] merrily

job to take your head off you so that we might kick it about the field since you were so impudent as to kick our ball. You must score a goal of shinny against me and the two-and-thirty scholars. If you get the victory, you shall be free; if we conquer you, every one of us will hit you a blow on the head with his shinny."

"Well," said Conall, "I do not know who you are, great man, but it seems to me that your judgment is evil. If every one of you were to give me a knock on the head, you would leave my head a soft mass. I have no shinny that I can play with."

"You shall have a shinny," said Gealbhan Greadhna.

Conall looked around, and he saw a crooked stick of elder growing on the face of a bank. He leaped over there and plucked it out by the root, and he sliced it with his sword and made a shinny.

Once he had fashioned the shinny, Conall and Gealbhan Greadhna went to play.

Two halves were made of the company, one half to play with the prince and the other to play with Conall. The ball was let out in the middle. Quickly, Conall got a chance at the ball; he struck it with a stroke of his foot, a blow of his palm, and a blow of his shinny, and he drove it home.

"You are impudent," said Gealbhan Greadhna, "to drive the game against me and my half of the people."

"That is well said by you, good lad! You shall get two-thirds of the group with you, and I will take one-third."

"And what will you say if it goes against you?"

"If it goes against me with fair play there is no help for it. But if it goes against me otherwise, I may say what I choose,"

Then divisions were made of the company, and Gealbhan Greadhna had two divisions and Conall one. The ball was let out in the middle, and, as it was let out, Conall got a chance at it, and he struck it with a stroke of his foot, a blow of his palm, and a blow of his shinny, and he drove it in.

"You are impudent," said Gealbhan Greadhna a second time, "to drive the game against me."

"Good lad, that is well from you! But you shall get the whole company the third time, and what will you say if it goes against you."

"If it goes by fair play I cannot say a jot," said Gealbhan Greadhna. "If not, I may say my pleasure."

The ball was let go and, again, Conall got a chance at it, and he was all alone, and he struck it with a stroke of his foot, a blow of his palm, and a blow of his shinny, and he drove it in.

"You are impudent," said Gealbhan Greadhna, "to go and drive it against me a third time."

"That is well from you, good lad, but you shall not say that to me, nor another man after me." And he struck him a blow with his shinny and knocked his brains out.

Conall looked contemptuously at the others. He threw his shinny aside and left.

He carried on his way and saw a little man coming laughing towards him.

"What is the meaning of your laughing at me?" said Conall.

Said the little man: "It is only that I am in a cheery mood at seeing a man of my country."

"Who are you," said Conall, "that is a countryman of mine?"

"I," said the little man, "am Duanach MacDraodh (songster, son of magic), the son of a prophet from Eirinn. "Will you then take me as your servant, lad?"

"I will take you," said Conall. "I have no way of surviving here without the guidance of a gillie.[83] What realm is this?"

"You are," said Duanach, "in the realm of Lochlann."

Conall went on and Duanach with him, and he saw a great town ahead.

"What town is there, Duanach?" said Conall.

"That," said Duanach, "is the great town of the realm of Lochlann."

They went on and they saw a big house on a high place.

"What big house is yonder, Duanach?"

---

[83] A man or boy who attends someone on a hunting, fishing or other expedition.

"That," said Duanach, "is the big house of the King of Lochlann." They went on. They saw another house in a high place.

"What pointed[84] house is there, Duanach?" said Conall.

"That is the house of the Tamhaisg[85], the best warriors that are in the realm of Lochlann," said Duanach.

"I heard my grandfather speaking about the Tamhaisg, but I have never seen them; I will visit them," said Conall.

"I would advise against that," said Duanach.

On he went to the palace of the King of Lochlann and, that his presence be known, he clashed his shield, summoning either battle should commence or Breast of Light should be delivered to him.

It turned out that he would get battle and not Breast of Light, daughter of the King of Laidheann, for she was not there to be given to him.

There would be no fighting at that time of night, but he would be given lodging in the house of the Tamhaisg, where there were eighteen hundred and eighteen Tamhaisg. The battle would commence in the morning at first light.

He went into the lodging and there was none of the Tamhaisg within who did not grin. When he saw that they had made a grin, he made two.

---

[84] suggesting palisades

[85] Among its several meanings, tamhaisg can be translated as "ghost, specter, apparition"—a suitably ominous term for the warriors in question.

"What is the meaning of your grinning at us?" said the Tamhaisg.

"What is the meaning of your grinning at me?" said Conall.

Said they: "Our grinning at you meant that your fresh royal blood will be ours to quench our thirst, and your fresh royal flesh ours to polish our teeth."

And said Conall: "The meaning of my grinning is that I will look out for the one with the biggest knob and slenderest shanks, and knock out the brains of the rest of you with that one."

Every one of them arose and went to the door and put a stake of wood against the door. Then Conall stood up and he put two stakes against the door—so tightly that the others fell.

"What reason had you to do that?" said they.

"What reason had you to do it?" said he. "It was a sorry matter for me that I should put two there when each one of you put one."

"Well, we will tell you," said they, "what our reason was. We long for a gulp of blood or a morsel of flesh, and you are the only one who has ever dared to come here. Oh, except for one other man, and he fled from us. And now everyone is worried that you will flee."

"Funny, that was the thing that made me do it as well—since I have you all here in one place. I feared I would have to be chasing you from hole to hole and from hill to hill if I did not bolt that door."

Then he gazed at them, one by one, and he seized on one of the slenderest shanks and the fattest head and he drove upon the rest, sliochd! slachd!—until he had killed every one of them. Nothing remained of the one he had used as a weapon, except the shank stump that was left in his hands.

He had killed every man of the Tamhaisg and, although he was such a youth as he was, he was utterly exhausted. Then he began tidying up the dwelling, cleaning it in readiness for his night there. He put outside all the carcasses of the dead in a heap. Then he stretched out on one of the beds that was within.

There came a dream upon him, telling him: "Rise, O Conall, an attack is about to be upon you."

He let that pass, and he gave it no heed, for he was exhausted.

The voice of the dream came again, and said to him, "Conall, will you not arise? A chase is about to be upon you."

He let that pass, and he gave it no heed; but the third time he came to him and said, "Conall, are you going to listen to me? Your life is in the gravest danger!"

He arose and he looked out at the door, and he saw a hundred carts, and a hundred horses, and a hundred carters, coming with food for the Tamhaisg. Supposing that the Tamhaisg had killed the youth that came amongst them the night before, a piper was playing music behind them, with joy and pleasure of mind.

They were coming over a single bridge, and the bridge was pretty large; and when Conall saw that they were together on the bridge, he raced to the bridge, and put each cart, and each horse, and each carter, over the bridge into the river; and he drowned all the men.

Word reached the young King of Lochlann, that the big man who came off the ocean had gone to the house of the Tamhaisg; that they had set to combat, and that the Tamhaisg had been slain.

The young King of Lochlann ordered four of the best warriors in his realm to go to the house of the Tamhaisg and take off the head of the big man who had come off the ocean. He wanted Conall's head brought to him by the time he sat down to his dinner.

The warriors left immediately. They found Duanach and they railed at him for assisting the big man that came from another land.

"And why," said Duanach, "should I not keep company with a man of my own country? But, to tell the truth, I am as tired of him as you are. He has given me much to do. You can see I have just sorted a heap of corpses, a heap of clothes, and a heap of the Tamhaisg arms. If you want any or all of that, you are welcome to take it along with you."

"It is not for that we came," said they, "but to slay him, and to take his head to the young King of Lochlann. Who is he?" said they.

"He is," said Duanach, "one of the sons of the King of Eirinn."

"The young King of Lochlann has sent us to cut his head off and to present it to him before he sits down to dinner," said they.

"If you kill one of the children of the King of Eirinn in his sleep you will regret it enough afterward," said Duanach.

"What regret will there be?" said they.

"There is this," said Duanach. "If you kill a clansman of the King of Eirinn in his sleep there will be no son to woman, there will be no calf to cow, no grass nor briard[86] shall grow in the realm of Lochlann, for seven years. Go and tell that to the young King of Lochlann."

They went back, and they told the king what Duanach had said.

The young King of Lochlann said that they should go back, and do as he had bidden them and that they should not heed the lies of Duanach. The four warriors went again to the house of the Tamhaisg, and they said to Duanach:

"We have come again to take the head off the son of the King of Eirinn."

And Duanach said: "He is yonder then, over there, sleeping. But take good heed to yourselves, unless your swords are sharp enough to take off his head at the first blow, all that is in your bodies is to be pitied after that. He will not leave one of you alive, and he will bring ruin to the realm."

Each of them stretched his sword to Duanach, and Duanach said that their swords were not sharp enough. He instructed them to go to the Tamhaisg stone to sharpen them. They went out, and they began sharpening their swords on the smooth grinding stone of the Tamhaisg.

Conall began to dream again. He was going on a road that went through the middle of a gloomy wood, and it seemed to him that he saw four lions before him, two on the upper side of the road, and two

---

[86] "braird" in the original. It may be a reference to a type of Scottish terrier called a briard.

on the lower side. They were gnashing their teeth, and swishing their tails, making ready to spring upon him.

It seemed to him that it was easier for the lions that were on the upper side of the road to leap down than it was for the lions that were on the lower side to leap up. Therefore, it was better for him to slay those that were on the upper side first. He gave a cheery spring to be at them, springing aloft in his sleep. In so doing, he struck his head against a tie beam that ran across the house of the Tamhaisg, and he drove as much as the breadth of a half-crown piece of skin off the top of his head. He was thus rudely awakened, and he said to Duanach:

"I was dreaming, Duanach," and he told him his dream.

And Duanach said: "Your dream is dainty to interpret. Go out to the stone of the Tamhaisg and you will see the four best warriors that the King of Lochlann has, two on each side of the stone, sharpening their swords to take off your head."

Conall went out with his blade in his hand and he took off their heads, and he left two heads on each side of the stone of the Tamhaisg and he returned to Duanach, and said:

"I am yet without food since I came to the realm of Lochlann, and I feel in myself that I am growing weak."

And Duanach said: "I will get you food if you will take my counsel, and that is, that you should go to court the sister of the King of Lochlann. I will go to ready the way for you."

There were three great warriors in the king's palace in search of the daughter of the King of Lochlann, and they sent word for the one who was the most valiant of them to go to combat the youth who had come to the town. This most valiant came, and the Amhus Ormanach[87] was his name. He and Conall were to try each other. They went and began the battle, Conall and the Amhus Ormanach.

The daughter of the King of Lochlann came to the door, and she shouted for Duanach Acha Draohd.

"I am here," said Duanach.

"Well, then, if you are, it is but little care you have for me. Many calving cattle and heifers were given by my father to your father. And yet you are not standing behind the Amhus Ormanach, and urging him on with the wisdom of a bard, so that he may bring the head of the wretch to me for my dinner. I have a great thirst for it."

"Faire![88] Faire! Watch, O princess[89]," said Duanach; "if you had quicker asked it, you had not got it slower."

Away went Duanach down, and it was not on the side of the Amhus Ormanach he placed himself but on the side of Conall.

"You have not told me for certain yet, if it is you, when you are not hastening thine hand and making heavy your blow! And to let slip that wretch that ought to be in a land of holes, or in crannies of rock, or in otter's cairns! Though you should fall here for slowness or

---

[87] At his first mention in the story, he is referred to as the Amhus Ormanach. In Gaelic, "amhus" means a hired soldier. Subsequent mentions refer dominantly to the man as "Avas Ormanach." I have preferred "Amhus" throughout, preceded by the definite article "the" (as is usual in the rest of the story).

[88] Watch!

[89] "queen" in the original but, as the daughter of the king, "princess" feels more appropriate.

slackness, there would neither be wife nor sweetheart crying for you, and that is not the like of what would befall him."[90]

Conall thought that it was in good purpose the man was for him, and not for an evil purpose. He put his sword under the sword of the Amhus Ormanach, and he cast it to the skies. Then he gave a spring on his back, and he leveled him on the ground. He prepared to take his head off.

"Subtle be your hand, O Conall," said Duanach Acha Draodh. "Tie him with the binding of the three smalls[91] until he gives you his oaths under the edge of his set of arms that he will never again strike a stroke against you."[92]

"I have not got ropes enough to bind him," said Conall.

"That is not my case," said Duanach. "I have enough rope to tie back-to-back everyone in the realm of Lochlann."

---

[90] Duanach has a wonderfully verbose, and confusing, way of arguing his point. Yes, he suggests, this scoundrel ought to lie dead in an otter's den but what good would that do? If you were to die at this point, he goes on living, and there would be no one to mourn you (since, of course, Conall has not yet recovered Breast of Light). By killing the Amhus, Duanach infers, you make an enemy of all who loved him. Conall thinks that Duanach means well by him but he does not quite get the point—perhaps because he is an assassin rather than a politician. It takes another more explicit intervention from Duanach, a few lines later, to make him realize that keeping the Amhus alive is the better strategy.

[91] The binding of the three smalls was a form of torture, involving the tying together and gradual tightening of the waist, ankles, and wrists.

[92] A "set of arms" is what we now call a coat of arms—it consists of the insignia and heraldic design of a monarch, which would have been emblazoned on a knight's shield and on his surcoat, the long coat he wore over his armor (hence the expression "a coat of arms"). In swearing an oath, a knight would place his hand below the heraldic image, and state the terms of the oath.

Duanach gave the rope to Conall, and Conall bound the Amhus Ormanach. He gave his oaths to Conall, under the edge of his set of arms, that he would be a loved comrade to him forever. He promised that he would only strike a stroke in support of him, and never against him. Conall thus spared the life of the Amhus Ormanach.

"You shall have that woman whom you are courting and making love to—the daughter of the King of Lochlann," said the Amhus Ormanach.

"You shall have that woman for yourself," said Conall. "It is not she whom I am seeking."

The daughter of the King of Lochlann was right well pleased that he had spared the life of the Amhus Ormanach so that he might be her own.

But what should the daughter of the King of Lochlann do but send word for Conall to pass the evening together with the queen and with herself? And if it were his will, for convenience he could be hauled up in a creel to the top of the castle.[93] Conall thought that if he did that it would be a bad look for someone from the realm of Eirinn to do that in the realm of Lochlann.

---

[93] A creel is a large wicker basket, usually for carrying fish. With a block and tackle, it can be used to transport people and materials up and down precipices or castle walls—as in another story in this anthology: "The Ridire of Grianaig and Iain the Soldier's Son." In the case of the present story, there is a hint of suspicion about the daughter of the King of Lochlan's suggestion, since it suggests a private entry to her room rather than the normative public entry (i.e. up a well-patrolled staircase).

Instead, he gave a spring from the small of his foot to the point of his palm, and from the point of his palm to the top of the castle, and he reached the woman where she was.

"If you are sore or injured," said the daughter of the King of Lochlann, "there is a vessel of balsam to wash yourself with, and you will be well after it."

He did not know if it was good or bad oil, so he put a little twig into the vessel to test what was in it. The twig came up as full of sap as it went down. He was persuaded that it was good oil.

He went and he washed himself in it, and he was as whole and healed as he had ever been. Then meat and drink were brought to them so that they might have pleasure of mind while passing the evening. After that, they went to rest; but he drew his cold sword between himself and the woman. He passed the night so and, in the morning, he rose and went out of the castle.

Then the daughter of the King of Lochlann called out. "Are you there, father?"[94]

"I am," said her father.

"Well," said she, "it is but little care you had of me. Why have you not brought me the head of that man who has made me a woman of

---

[94] She calls upon her "brother" to exact retribution. But she must mean her father, since it is he who fights Conall and he who later agrees that, in exchange for Conall sparing his life, the realm of Lochlann will be under cess (i.e. payment of a tribute tax) to Conall—to which only the monarch of the realm could agree. She cannot call for her husband-to-be, the Amhus Ormanach, to defend her honor since he has already sworn an oath that he will never strike a blow at Conall who has spared his life on exactly that condition.

harrying and hurrying[95], and to whom I fell as a wedded wife last night. Bring his head to my breakfast. I am greatly thirsting for it."[96]

"Faire! Faire! Watch, oh daughter," said he. "If you had asked it sooner you had not got it slower. There is no man, small or great, in Christendom who will turn back my hand."

He went, and before he reached the door, he set the earth quaking seven miles from him. At the first growl he gave after he got out of the castle, there was no cow in calf, or mare in foal, or woman with child, that did not suffer for fear.

He and Conall began the battle. They drew their slender gray swords, and battled from the rising of the sun until the evening, when she would be wending west; and without knowing who would win or who would lose.

Duanach was singing iolla[97] to them. Then the daughter of the King of Lochlann cried out for Duanach acha Draodh that he should go down to give the urging of a true wise bard to her father. She urged him also to bring her the head of the wretch to her breakfast because she was thirsting greatly for it.

---

[95] "harrying and hurrying"—she articulates a process of bullying and coercion to explain how she became his "wedded wife." The narrator infers this may be untrue since, we are told, Conor placed his "cold sword" between them to prevent any kind of liaison—but that proves nothing since we can never know what happened in that castle chamber.

[96] It seems odd that having spared her husband-to-be, the daughter of the King of Lochlan once again demands Conall's head on a platter. Oral narrations are fond of recurring plot loops, with repetitive sentence and paragraph structures, since these allow for extending presentations with an economy of memorization.

[97] Merrily—there is a long tradition of song and music being used to inspire soldiers on the battlefield.

Duanach went, and if he did, it was not to the back of the King of Lochlann he went, but behind Conall.

"O Conall," said Duanach, "you have not told it to me for certain yet, if it is you, when you are not hastening thine hand and making heavy your blow! And to let slip that wretch who ought to be in a land of holes, or in crannies of rock, or in otter's cairns! Though you should fall here for slowness or slackness, there would neither be wife nor sweetheart crying for you, and that is not the like of what would befall him."

Conall thought that it was in good purpose the man was for him, and that it was not in bad purpose. He put his sword under the sword of the King of Lochlann, and he cast it to the skies, and then he gave a spring himself on his back, and he leveled him on the ground, and he prepared to take off his head.

"Let your hand be subtle, Conall," said Duanach. "Little is his little shambling head worth to you."

Said Conall to Duanach: "Pass my sword to me, so I may take off his head."

"Not I, indeed," said Duanach. "It is better for you to have his head for yourself as it is than to have five hundred heads that you might sever with strife. Make him promise that he will be a friend to you."

Conall made the young King of Lochlann promise with words and heavy vows, that he would be a friend to Conall Guilbeanach, the son of the King of Eirinn, in each strait or extremity that might come upon him, whether the matter should come with right or wrong; and that Conall should have the realm of Lochlann under cess.[98]

When the King of Lochlann had given these promises, Conall let him up and they caught each other by the hand and made peace.

And the King of Lochlann requested of Conall that he should come in with him to his Great House to dine with him. The king ordered a double watch upon the occasion so that no one should disturb him or the young son of the King of Eirinn while they were at their feast.

A churchman was found, and the Amhus Ormanach was married to the daughter of the King of Laidheann.

When each thing was ready the royal ones sat down at the great board. They laid down lament, and they raised up music with rejoicing and great joy, and they were in great pleasure of mind. Meat was set in the place for eating, drink in the drinking place, music in the place for hearing; and they were plying the feast with great sport in the dining room of the King of Lochlann.

The soldiers were outside watching, guarding the big house of the king when they saw a huge giant coming their way. They had such fear before him that they thought they could see the great world between his legs.

As he was coming nearer, the watch were fleeing until they reached the great house. The intruder ran into the main passage and from the passage into the hall where the young King of Lochlann and the young son of the King of Eirinn were at their feast. The great raw bones[99] began to chain and bind the men and cast them behind him until he had bound every one of them.

---

[98] Tax. In other words a regular levy would have to be paid to Conall.

[99] the intruder

He reached the young King of Lochlann, and he and the big man wrestled with each other. He drew his fist and he struck the King of Lochlann between the mouth and nose, and he drove out three front teeth, and he caught them on the back of his fist. The young King of Lochlann was bound and laid under fetters, and thrown behind together with the rest. Then the big man gave a dark leap and he seized the bride and took her with him.

Conall gazed on all the company that was within, to see if any man would rise to stand by the king. When he saw no one stepping forward, he stepped forward himself.

"Let that woman go," said he. "You have no business with her." The giant refused. Conall gave a spring and caught the big man between the two sides of the door, and he leveled him. And once he had leveled him, he let the weight of his knee rest on his chest.

"Has death ever gone so near you as that?" said Conall.

"It has gone nearer than that," said the big man.

He put more weight on him. "Has death gone as near as that to you?"

"Oh, he has not gone that near; let your knee be lightened, and I will tell you the time that he went nearest to me."

"I will let you tell your story," said Conall.

Conall loosed the young King of Lochlann and his men from their bonds and their fetters. He sat himself and the young King of Lochlann at the board, and they took their feast, and the big man was cast in under the board.

When they were at supper the king's sister was with them, and every word she said she was trying to make the friendship greater and greater between her brother and Conall.

The big man was lying under the board and Conall said to him:

"You, man, that is beneath, were you ever before in strait or extremity as great as to be lying under the great board, under the drippings of the waxen torches of the King of Lochlann and mine?"

Said be, "If I were above, a comrade of meat and cup to you, I would tell you a tale on that."

At the end of a while after that, when the drink was taking Conall a little, he was willing to hear the tale of the man who was beneath the board, and he said to him:

"You that are beneath the board, whatever your name is, were you ever in a trait or extremity as great as this?

And he answered as before.

Said Conall, "If you will promise to be peaceable when you get up, I will let you come up; and if you are not peaceable, the two hands that put you down before will put you down again."

Conall loosed the man who was beneath, and he rose aloft and sat at the other side of the board, opposite to Conall; and Conall said:

"Aha! you are on high now, you man that was beneath. If I had your name, it is that I would call you.[100] What strait or extremity were you

---

[100] "If I had your name"—we should accept this as a general challenge to any other

ever in that was harder than to be laid under the board of the young king of Lochlann, and mine?"

---

storyteller in the vicinity (whatever his, her, or their name may be) to step up and tell a better story of extremity than this. The next story in this anthology, "Story of the King of Spain," is a direct riposte to the challenge.

STORY OF THE KING OF SPAIN

Said he: "My name is Garna Sgiathlais Righ na Iospainde (Garna Skeelance, King of Spain).[101]

Let me tell you about the toughest situation in which I ever found myself."

I was once a warrior, and the deeds of a warrior were on my hands well enough. I was on my way to the dun[102] of the King of Laidheann to capture Breast of Light with a right strong hand.

I saw Mac a-Mor, son of the king of the Sorcha, and the most beauteous woman that I ever saw upon his shoulder. I never saw a woman that I would rather wish to have for myself than that woman. I menaced and taunted him with my sword, flicking as high as the band of his kilt. He had only one song for me:

"Will you not cease, and will you not stop?" But I paid no attention to him.

Then he fell upon me and bound me, and fettered me, and set me on a horse before him. He took me to the top of a rock. The rock was high, and he threw me down the rock, and if I had fallen to the

---

[101] This story is effectively a continuation of "The Story of Conall Guilbeanach," narrated by John MacNair and written down by John Dewar at a point in the 1850s.
[102] fortress or castle

bottom I would have been smashed to pieces. But, by chance, fell into the nest of a dreagan.[103]

When I came to myself, I looked about me, and I saw three great birds in the nest. I held my hands and my feet to them, as they were bound until they pecked at the bindings and loosened them; the monsters! They might just as easily have torn me asunder.

I saw a cave at the back of the nest, and I dragged myself into the cave, and when the old dreagan would come and leave food for the young ones, I would stay until she left, and then I would come out and I would steal the food from the young dreagans. That was all I had to keep me alive.

In the end, the young dreagans died for want of food. The old dreagan realized that something had been eating their food, and she ransacked all about the nest—and then she went into the cave.

She saw me and seized me in her talons; she sailed on the back of the ocean with me; and then she sprang to the clouds with me. For a time, I had no idea which was heaven or earth for me, nor whether she would let me fall in the drowning sea, or on hard rocks, or on cairns of stones.

Then she kept lifting me and letting me fall until at last she saw that I was floating dead on the breast of the sea. Though I was not heavy at first, the weight of my brine-soaked body became heavy indeed; and the lifting and dropping of me exhausted her. Finally, she plucked my dead body from the surface of the sea and she sailed with me to an island. She put me on the sunny side of the island. Because the sun was so hot, sleep came upon her and she dozed off.

---

[103] This is a monstrously large mythical bird.

The sun also had a curiously enlivening effect on me, even though I was dead.

She had landed at the side of a well and, when she awoke, she began splashing about in the well. I realized that there was a healing elixir in the well because the side of me that was nearest to the well was healing with the splashes of water that the dreagan was putting about the place. And I moved the other side of my body towards the well until that side was healed also.

Then I felt for my sword which had always stuck by me. I found it, rose, and crept softly up behind the dreagan. With the sword, I struck off her head with a simple blow. But the healing balsam that was in the well was so strong that although her head had been cut off it kept springing back on. Finally, I placed the sword between the head and the neck of the monstrous bird and held on until the hag's marrow froze. At last, the head and the neck were fully driven asunder.

I did not leave a shred of her uncut until her blood had spread and dried throughout the island. And when the blood had dried, I put the dreagan into the well, and then I jumped in and washed myself in it. I seemed to grow stronger and more active than I had ever been before.

My first exploit after that was to battle against the King of Lochlann, and it would not have gone well for me without that extra power.

And so, in my opinion, being cast into the nest of the dreagan, and what I went through before escaping with my life, is a harder strait and a worse extremity, in my esteem, than to be under the board of the King of Lochlann.

THE DAUGHTER OF THE SKIES

Once upon a time, there was a farmer, and he had a leash of daughters, and many cattle and sheep.[104] He went on a day to see them, and none of them were to be found, and he took the length of the day to search for them. He saw, in the lateness, coming home, a little doggy running about a park.

The doggy came to where he was.

"What will you give me," said the dog, "if I round up your herds of cattle and sheep for you?"

"I do not know, you ugly thing. What will you be asking for? I will give it to you if it is anything I have."

"Will you give me," said the dog, "your big daughter to marry?"

"I will give her to you," said he, "if she will take you herself."

They went home, himself and the dog. Her father asked the eldest daughter if she would accept the doggy. She said she would not. He asked the second one if she would marry him, and she said she would not marry him even if it meant the cattle should remain left out forever.

He asked the youngest one if she would marry the doggy, and she said she would marry him. They married, and her sisters mocked her

[104] The story is attributed to James MacLauchlan, a servant from Islay in the mid-nineteenth century.

because she had married a dog.

He took her with him and headed home. When he came to his dwelling place, he changed into a splendid man. After they had been together a great time, she said she had better go to visit her father. He asked her to take care that she should not stay until she gave birth, for she was then expecting. She said she would not stay long enough for that to happen.

Her husband gave her a steed. He told her that, as soon as she reached the house, she should take the bridle from the horse's head and let her run away. And when she wished to come home, she only had to shake the bridle, and the steed would come and place her head into the bridle.

She did as he asked her. She was not long at her father's house when she fell ill, and a child was born. That night men were on watch together around a fire. There came the prettiest music that ever was heard about the town, and everyone within slept but she.

Her husband came in and he took the child from her. He left and he went away. The music stopped, and each one awoke, and there was no knowing where the child had gone.

She did not say anything, but so soon as she rose, she took with her the bridle and shook it, and the steed came and put her head into it. She took herself off riding, but the steed took to going home; and the swift March wind that would be before her, she would catch; and the swift March wind that would be after her, could not catch her.

She arrived.

"You are come," said he.

"I came," said she. He mentioned nothing to her and no more did she mention anything to him. Around nine months later, again she said: "I had better go see my father." He said to her about this journey as he had said before. She took the steed and rode away. When she arrived, she took the bridle from the steed's head, and she sent her home.

That very night a child was born. Her husband came as he did before, with music; everyone slept, and he took the child with him. When the music stopped, they all awoke. Her father was standing before her face, demanding that she tell him what was going on. She would not say anything. When she was well, she rose and took with her the bridle. She shook it and the steed came and put her head into it. She took herself away home.

When she arrived, he said:

"You have come."

"I came," said she. He mentioned nothing to her; no more did she mention anything to him.

Again, at the end of nine months, she said: "I had better go to see my father."

"Yes," said he, "but take care you do not do as you did on the other two journeys."

"I will not," said she. He gave her the steed and she went away.

She reached her father's house, and that very night a child was born. The music came as was usual, and the child was taken away. Then her father was before her face, and he was going to kill her if she would not tell what was happening to the children; or what sort of man she had married.

With the fright he gave her, she told him the full story. When she grew well, she took the bridle with her to a hill that was nearby, and she began shaking the bridle to see if the steed would come and put her head into it. But shake as she may, the steed would not come. When she saw that she was not coming, she went out on foot. When she arrived at her husband's home, no one was within but the crone[105] that was his mother.

"You are without a houseman today," said the crone. "But if you are quick, you may yet catch him." She went off and carried on searching until night came on her. She saw then a light in a dwelling a long way from her; and though it was a long way from her, she was not long in reaching it.

When she went in she saw the floor had been swept before her arrival, and a housewife was spinning up at the far end of the house.

"Come up," said the housewife. "I know of your cheer and travel. You are going to see if you can catch your man. He is going to marry the daughter of the King of the Skies."

"He is!" exclaimed she.

The housewife rose she made meat for her. She brought water to wash her feet, and she laid her down. If the day came quickly, it was quicker still that the housewife arose, and that the housewife made

---

[105] In folklore, a crone is an old woman who may be characterized as disagreeable, malicious, or sinister in manner, often with magical or supernatural associations that can make her either helpful or obstructive.

breakfast for her. She prepared her for departure on foot, and she gave her shears[106] that would cut by themselves and said to her:

"You will be in the house of my middle sister tonight."

She traveled and traveled until night came and she had still not reached the house of the housewife's middle sister. Then she saw a light a long way from her; and if it was a long way from her, she was not long in reaching it. When she went into the house she saw it was already swept, with a fire in the middle of the floor, and the housewife spinning at the end of the room.

"Come up," said the housewife. "I know your cheer and travel."

She made meat for her, she brought water, she washed her feet, and she laid her down. No sooner came the day than the housewife woke up the young woman, and made breakfast for her. She said she had better go, and she gave her a needle that would sew by itself.

"You will be in the house of my youngest sister tonight," said she. She traveled and traveled until the end of the day and the mouth of lateness. She saw a light a long way from her; and if it was a long way from her, she was not long in reaching it. She went in, the house was swept, and the housewife spinning at the end of the fire.

"Come up," said she. "I know of your cheer and travel." She made meat for her, she brought water, she washed her feet, and she laid her down.

If the day came quickly, it was quicker still that the housewife rose; she woke her up, and made her breakfast; she gave her a clue[107] of

---

[106] Scissors.

thread. The thread would go into the eye of the needle by itself, and as the shears would cut, and the needle sewed, the thread would always keep up with them.

"You will be in the town tonight," said the housewife. She reached the town about evening, and she went into the house of the king's henwife[108] to lay down her weariness and warm herself at the fire. She asked the crone to give her work because she would rather be working than be still.

"No man is doing a turn in this town today," says the henwife. "The king's daughter has a wedding."

"Ud!" said she to the crone. "Give me cloth to sew, or a shirt that will keep my hands going." The crone gave her shirts to make. She took the shears from her pocket, and she set it to work. She set the needle to work after it; as the shears would cut, the needle would sew, and the thread would go into the needle by itself. One of the king's servant maids came in. She was watching her, and it caused her great wonder how she made the shears and the needle work by themselves. She went home and told the king's daughter that someone was in the house of the henwife and that she had shears and a needle that could work by themselves.

"If there is," said the king's daughter, "go you over in the morning, and ask her what she would accept for the shears."

In the morning she went over, and she said that the king's daughter was asking what would she take for the shears.

---

[107] A ball of yarn or thread
[108] The henwife is not the keeper of hens (!) but, rather, a wise old woman who is often an herbalist or a healer

"Nothing I would ask," said she, "except permission to lie where she lay last night."

"Go back again," said the king's daughter, "and tell her that she will get that." She gave the shears to the king's daughter.

When they went to lie down, the king's daughter gave her man a sleep drink, so that he might not wake. He did not wake the length of the night. No sooner came the day, than the king's daughter came where she was, got her onto her feet, and put her out the door.

The following day she was working with the needle, and cutting with other shears. The king's daughter sent the maid servant over, and she asked "What would she take for the needle?" She said she would not take anything, except permission to lie where she lay last night. The maid-servant told this to the king's daughter.

"She will get that," said the king's daughter. The maid-servant reported this to the young woman, and the king's daughter got the needle. When they were going to lie down, the king's daughter gave her man a sleep drink, and he did not wake that night.

The man's eldest son was lying in a bed beside his father and the young woman, and he heard her speaking to him through the night, and saying to him that she was the mother of his three children. The next morning he and his father were taking a walk outside, and he told his father what he had heard.

That same day the king's daughter sent the servant maid to ask what she would take for the clue, and she said she would ask permission to lie where she lay last night.

"She will get that," said the king's daughter. On this night when the man got the sleep drink, he emptied it and he did not drink it at all.

Through the night she said to him that he was the father of her three sons, and he said that he was. In the morning, when the king's daughter came down, he asked her to go back upstairs and said that the young woman who was with him was, in fact, his wife. When they rose, they left to go home. They arrived home, the spells wore off him, they set up home together, and I left them and they left me.

THE DAUGHTER OF KING UNDERWAVES

On a wild night, the Fhinn people were together on the side of Beinn Eudainn.[109] There was pouring rain and falling snow from the north. About midnight a creature of uncouth appearance hammered at the door of Fionn. Her hair was down to her heels, and she cried to him to let her in under the border of his covering. Fionn raised up a corner of the covering, and he gazed at her.

"You strange-looking ugly creature," said he. "Your hair is down to your heels; how could you ask me to let you in?"

She went away and she gave a scream. She reached Oisean, and she asked him to let her in under the border of his covering. Oisean lifted a corner of his covering and he saw her.

"You strange, hideous creature, how can you ask me to let you in?" said he. "Your hair is down to your heels. You shall not come in."

She went away and she gave a shriek.

She reached Diarmaid, and she cried aloud to him to let her in under the border of his covering. Diarmaid lifted a fold of his covering, and he saw her.

"You are a strange, hideous creature," he said. "Your hair is down to your heels, but come in." She came in under the border of his

---

[109] John Francis Campbell in *Popular Tales of the West Highlands* cites Roderick MacLean, a tailor of Ken Tangval, Barra, as the source of this tale. MacLean reported hearing it from old men in South Uist, including Angus Macintyre who lived at Bornish and was around eighty years old.

covering.

"Oh, Diarmaid," said she, "I have spent seven years traveling over ocean and sea, and of all that time I have not passed a night until this night when you have let me in. Let me come into the warmth of the fire."

"Come up to the fire," said Diarmaid.

When she came up to the fire, the people of the Fhinn began to flee, so hideous was she.

"Go to the further side," said Diarmaid, "and let the creature come to the warmth of the fire."

They went to the other side, and they let her be at the fire. But she had not been long at the fire when she sought to be under the warmth of the blanket together with himself.

"You are growing too bold," said Diarmaid. "First you asked to come under the border of the covering, then you sought to come to the fire, and now you ask leave to come under the blanket with me. But come."

She went under the blanket, and he turned a fold of it between them. She was not long thus when he gave a start, and he gazed at her, and he saw at his side the finest woman who ever lived, from the beginning of the universe to the end of the world. He shouted out to the rest to come over where he was, and he said to them.

"It is not often that men are unkind! Is not this the most beautiful woman that man ever saw!"

"She is," said they, as they covered her up, "the most beautiful woman that man ever saw."

She went to sleep and did not know that they were still looking at her. Diarmaid let her sleep and did not awaken her when he woke in the night. But a short time after that she awoke.

"Are you awake Diarmaid?" she asked him.

"I am awake," said Diarmaid.

"If you could have the very finest castle you have ever seen, where would you have it built?"

"Up above Beinn Eudainn, if I had my choice," said Diarmaid and he went to sleep, and she said no more to him.

Someone went out riding early, before daylight, and he saw a castle built up on the hill. He cleared his sight to see if it was actually there; then he saw it was real, and he went home but he did not say a word.

Another went out, and he saw it, and he did not say a word. Then the day brightened, and the two came in saying that the castle was most surely there. Said she, as she sat up: "Arise Diarmaid, go up to your castle, and be not stretched here any longer."

"If there were a castle to which I might go, I would go," said he.

"Look out and see if there is a castle there."

He went outside and saw a castle, and came back in. I will go up to the castle if you will go there with me."

"I will do that, Diarmaid, but say not to me three times how you did find me," said she.

"I will not say to you ever how I found you," said Diarmaid.

They went to the castle, the pair of them. What a beautiful castle! There was nothing needed by a castle that was not provided for—there was even a gaggle of geese. The meat was on the board, and there were maid servants and men servants about it.

They spent three days in the castle together and, at the end of three days, she said to him: "You are turning sorrowful because you are not together with the rest of your people."

"Don't think I am feeling sorrow because I am not together with the Fhinn," said he.

"You had best go with the Fhinn, and your meat and your drink will be no worse than here," said she.

"Who will take care of the greyhound bitch and her three pups?" said Diarmaid.

"Oh," said she, "what fear is there for the greyhound and the three pups?"

When he heard that, he went away. He left a blessing with her, and he reached the people of the Fhinn and saw Fionn, the brother of his mother. There was a chief's honor and welcome for Diarmaid when he arrived. Some had ill will towards him because the woman had come first to them, and they had turned their backs on her. And because he had followed her wishes and the matter had turned out so well for him.

She was outside after he had gone away, and what should she see but someone coming in great haste? She decided to stay outside until he arrived, and who came there but Fionn? He hailed her and caught her by the hand.

"You are angry with me, damsel," said he.

"Oh, I am not at all, Fionn," said she. "Come in and take a draught from me."

"I will go if I get my request," said Fionn.

"What request might there be that you wouldn't get?" said she.

"Just this—one of the pups of the greyhound bitch."

"Oh, the request you have asked is not great," said she. "The one you may choose, take it with you."

He chose one and he went away.

Diarmaid came in the early evening. The greyhound met him outside, and she gave a yelp.

"It is true, my lass, one of your pups is gone. But if you had remembered how I found you, how your hair was down to your heels, you would not have let the pup go."

"Diarmaid, why do you speak like that?"

"Oh," said Diarmaid, "I ask forgiveness."

"Oh, you shall get that," said she and he slept in the castle that night, and his meat and drink were as usual.

In the morning, he went to where he was the day before, and while he was gone, she went out to take a stroll. While she was walking along, what should she see but a rider coming to where she was? She stayed outside until he reached her.

Who reached her here but Oisean, son of Fionn.

They gave welcome and honor to each other. She told him to go in with her, and that he should take a draught from her. He said that he would if he might get his request.

"What request have you?" said she.

"One of the pups of the greyhound bitch."

"You shall get that," said she. "Take your choice of them."

He took the pup with him, and he went away.

At the opening of the night came Diarmaid home, and the greyhound met him outside, and she gave two yelps.

"That is true, my lass," said Diarmaid to the greyhound, "another is taken from you. But if she had remembered how I found her, when her hair was down to her heels, she would not have let one of your pups go."

"Diarmaid! What did you say there?" said she.

"I ask your pardon," said Diarmaid.

"You shall get that," said she, and they seized each other's hands, and they went inside together, and there was meat and drink that night as there ever had been.

In the morning Diarmaid went away, and after he had gone she took a stroll. She saw another rider coming and he was in great haste. She thought she would wait, and not go home until he arrived. What was this but another of the Fhinn?

He went with civil words to the young damsel, and they gave welcome and honor to each other.

She invited him to come up to the castle and take a draught from her. He said that he would go if he should get his request. She asked what that request might be.

"One of the pups of the greyhound bitch," said he.

"Though it is a hard matter for me," said she, "I will give it to you."

He went with her to the castle and took a draught from her. He collected the pup and he went away.

At the opening of the night, Diarmaid returned. The greyhound met him, and she gave three yelps, the most hideous that man ever heard.

"Yes, that is true my lass, you are without any this day," said Diarmaid, "but if she had a mind of how I found her when her hair was down to her heels, she would not have let the pup go. She would not have done that to me."

"You, Diarmaid, what did you say?"

"Oh, I am asking pardon," said Diarmaid. That night, there was no wife or bed beside him, as there had been before. It was in a moss hole he awoke on the following morning. There was no castle, nor a stone left of it. He began to weep, and he said to himself that he would not pause, head or foot, until he had found his lost woman.

Away he went, and what should he do but take his way across the glens? There was neither house nor ember to be seen. He gave a glance over his shoulder, and what should he see but the greyhound lying dead? He seized her by the tail and put her on his shoulder, and he would not part with her for the great love that he bore her.

He continued on his way, and what should he see ahead of him but a herder?

"Did you see, this day or yesterday, a woman traveling this way?" said Diarmaid to the herder.

"I saw a woman early in the morning yesterday, and she was walking hard," said the herder.

"What way did you see her going?"

"She went down yonder point to the strand, and I saw her no more."

He took the very road that she took until there was no going any further. He saw a ship. He put the slender end of his spear under his chest, and he sprang into her, and he went to the other side.[110] He laid himself down, stretched out on the side of a hill, and he slept. When he awoke there was no ship to be seen.

"A man to be pitied am I," said he. "I shall never get away from here, but there is nothing I can do."

He sat on a knoll, and he had not sat there long when he saw a boat coming with a man rowing it.

---

[110] This unusual skill is the same as that practiced by the hero in "The Story of Conall Guilbeanach" earlier in this anthology.

He went down to the boat but when it arrived it was empty. He grasped the greyhound by the tail and he put her in, and he climbed in after her.

Then the boat went out over the sea, and she went up and down in the water, and as it did he caught sight of land and a plain on which he could walk. He managed to get to shore and continued on his way.

He was only a short time walking when he came across a gulp of blood on the ground. He lifted the blood and he put it into a napkin, and he put the napkin into his pouch. "It was the greyhound that lost this," said he.

He walked a little further before he came across the next gulp of blood. He lifted it and put it into his pouch. He came across another and did the same with it.

After that, what should he see a short space from him but a woman gathering rushes as though she were crazed? He went towards her, and he asked her if she had any news she could give him.

"I cannot tell until I gather the rushes," said she.

"You could tell me while you are gathering," said Diarmaid.

"I am in great haste," said she.

"What place is here?" said he.

"This is," said she, "the Realm of the Underwaves."

"The Realm of the Underwaves?"

"Yes," said she.

"What use do you have for the rushes after you have gathered them?" said Diarmaid.

"The daughter of King Underwaves has come home. She was seven years under spells, and she is ill. The finest leech surgeons of Christendom are gathered, and none is doing her any good but a bed of rushes is what she finds the most comforting thing."

"Well then, I would be far in your debt if you would show me where that woman is." Surely, he thought, this was his woman!

"Well then, I can arrange that. I will put you into the sheaf of rushes, and I will put the rushes under you and over you, and I will take you with me on my back."

"That is a thing that surely you cannot do?" said Diarmaid.

"Leave that to me," said she.

She put Diarmaid into the bundle, and she took him on her back. When she reached the chamber, she let down the bundle.

"Oh! Hasten that to me," said the daughter of King Underwaves.

Diarmaid sprang out of the bundle and he sprang to meet her, and they seized each other's hands and there was joy then.

"Three parts of the ailment are gone, but I am still not well, and I will not be. Every time I thought of you when I was coming, I lost a gulp of the blood of my heart."

"Well then, I have got these three gulps of your heart's blood, take you them in a drink, and there will be nothing amiss," he said

"Well then, I will not take them," said she. "They will not do me a shade of good, since I cannot have the one thing I need, and I shall never get that in the world."

"What thing is that?" said he.

"There is no good in telling you that; you will not get it, nor any man in the world. It has discomfited them for so long."

"If it be on the surface of the world I will get it, just tell me what it is," said Diarmaid.

"I must get three draughts from the cup of the King of the Plain of Wonder, and no man has ever got that, and I shall not get it."

"Oh!" said Diarmaid, "there are not on the surface of the world enough people to keep it from me. Tell me if that man is far from here."

"He is not; he is within a bound near my father. A rivulet is there, and on it a sailing ship with the wind behind her. You must sail for a year and a day before you reach your destination."[111]

He went away and he reached the rivulet, and he spent a good while walking at its side.

---

[111] When the Dairmaid's beloved tells him that the King of the Plain of Wonder is not far away, we may think that traveling for a year and a day is something of an underestimation on her part. However, when we put this in the context of other great mythic journeys (Odysseus' 10 years' struggle to get home after the Trojan War; Hercules' 12 Labors during his 10 years of enforced servitude with King Eurystheus; Aeneas' harrowing seven-year journey to find a suitable place to establish Rome), Diarmaid's task is a relative shoo-in.

"I cannot cross over it," said Diarmaid to himself.

Before he had let the word out of his mouth, there stood a little russet man in the middle of the rivulet.

"Diarmaid, son of Duibhne, you are in trouble," said he.

"I am in trouble at this moment," said Diarmaid.

What would you give to a man who would bring you out of these straits? Come here and put your foot on my palm."

"Oh! My foot cannot go into your palm," said Diarmaid.

"It can."

He went and he put his foot on his palm. "Now, Diarmaid, it is to the King of the Plain of Wonder that you are going?"

"Indeed," said Diarmaid.

"You are going to seek his cup. I will come with you myself."

"You shall come," said Diarmaid.

Diarmaid reached the house of the King of the Plain of Wonder. He shouted for the cup to be sent out and, if the cup was not sent out, battle or combat would follow.

There were sent out four hundred Lugh Gaisgich, and four hundred Lan Gaisgich, and in two hours he left not a man of them alive.

He shouted again for battle or else combat, or the cup to be sent out.

That was the thing he would get, battle or else combat, and it was not the cup.

There were sent out eight hundred Lugh Gaisgich, and eight hundred Lan Gaisgich, and in three hours he left not a man of them alive.[112]

He shouted again for battle or else combat, or else the cup to be sent out to him.[113]

There were sent out nine hundred strong heroes, and nine hundred full heroes, and in four hours he left no man of them alive.

"From where," said the king as he stood in his great door, "has come the man who has just brought my realm to ruin? If it is the pleasure of the hero, let him tell us from where he came."

"It is the pleasure of the hero to do so. I am a hero of the people of the Fhinn. I am Diarmaid."

"Why did you not send in a message to say who it was? I would not have spent my realm upon you had I known. It was prophesied seven years before you were born that you would kill every man put against you. What do you require?"

"I require the cup; it comes from your hand for healing."

---

[112] Lugh Gaisgich were strong warriors, and Lan Gaisgich were champion warriors. A version of the ancient rankings of warriors is described in the original version of "The Story of Conall Guilbeanach." See Note 52.

[113] In technical terms, the difference between battle and combat seems straightforward: a battle is a full-scale engagement between armies; combat is a fight between individuals or small groups. In this case, though, we have a contest between an individual and an army. The narrator's uncertainty is understandable.

"No man ever got my cup but it is easy for me to give it to you."

Diarmaid got the cup from the King of the Plain of Wonder.

"I will now send a ship with you Diarmaid," said the king.

"Great thanks to you, O king. I am much in your debt, but I have a ferry of my own."

Here the king and Diarmaid parted from each other. He remembered when he had parted from the king that he had never said a word at all about the little russet man, and that he had not taken him in to meet the king. It was when he was coming near the rivulet that he thought of him, and he did not know how he should get over the river.

"There is no help for it," said he. "I shall not now get over on the ferry, and shame will not let me return to the king."

What should rise while the word was in his mouth but the little russet man out of the burn?

"You are in dire straits, Diarmaid."

"I am."

"It is this day that you are in extremity."

"It is. I won the thing I desired but I cannot get across the river."

"Despite doing to me all the things you have done, and despite not saying a word of me yesterday—yet, you may put your foot on my palm and I will take you over the burn."

Diarmaid put his foot on his palm, and he took him over the burn.

"You will talk to me now Diarmaid," said he.

"I will do it," said Diarmaid.

"You are going to heal the daughter of King Underwaves; she is the girl that you like best in the world."

"Oh! It is she."

"You shall go to a certain well. You will find a bottle at the side of the well, and you shall take it with you full of the well water. When you reach the damsel, you shall put the water in the cup, and a gulp of blood in it, and she will drink it. You shall fill it again, and she will drink. You shall fill it the third time, and you shall put the third gulp of blood into it, and she will drink it. And at that point, there will not be a thing ailing her. When you have given her the last, and she is well, she will be the person you care least about among all those you have ever seen before."

"Oh, not she!" said Diarmaid aghast.

"She will be. The king will know that you have taken a dislike to her. She will say Diarmaid, you have taken a dislike to me. Say that you have. Do you know what man is speaking to you?" said the little russet man.

"Not I," said Diarmaid.

"In me there is the messenger of the other world, who helped you; because your heart is so warm to do good to another. King Underwaves will come, and he will offer you much silver and gold for healing his daughter. You shall not take a thing. Ask only that the king should send a ship with you to Eirinn, to the place from where you came."

Diarmaid left. He reached the well; he got the bottle, and he filled it with water; he took it with him, and he reached the castle of King Underwaves. When he came in, he was honored and saluted.

"No man ever won that cup before," said she.

"I would have won it from all that there are on the surface of the world; there was no man who could turn me back," said Diarmaid.

"I thought that you would not get it though you were determined to go, but I see that you have it," said she.

He put a gulp of blood into the water in the cup, and she drank it. She drank the second one, and she drank the third one, and when she had drunk the third one there was not a jot ailing her. She was whole and healthy. When she was thus well, he took a dislike to her; scarcely could he bear to see her.

"Oh! Diarmaid," said she, "you are taking a dislike to me."

"Oh! I am," said he.

Then the king sent word throughout the town that she was healed, and music was raised, and lament laid down. The king came where Diarmaid was, and he said to him:

"Now, you shall take so much by counting of silver for healing her, and you shall have her in marriage."

"I will not take the damsel; and I will not take anything but a ship to be sent with me to Eirinn, where the Fhinn are gathered."

A ship went with him, and he reached the Fhinn and the brother of his mother, and there was great joy and pleasure that he had returned.

Printed in Great Britain
by Amazon

38a358b5-fe03-4cea-bf0a-7c88a5d4716dR02